SINGLE WIDE FEMALE

THE BUCKET LIST - BOOKS 1-6

LILLIANNA BLAKE

CONTENTS

THE BUCKET LIST

Twenty-Four Bold Challenges.

One Woman in Progress

#1 Learn Pole Dancing

#2 Start a Blog

#3 Learn to Cook

#4 Create a Masterpiece

#5 Run a Marathon

#6 Go Skinny Dipping

#7 Start Online Dating

#8 Learn Yoga

#9 Be a Mentor

#10 Crash a Wedding

#11 Be a Movie Extra

#12 Join a Writing Group

#13 Enjoy a Spa Day

#14 Donate Blood

#15 Learn Poker

#16 Get a Tattoo

#17 Host a Dinner Party

#18 Publish a Book

#19 Walk Across Hot Coals

#20 Learn to Swim

#21 Learn to Meditate

#22 Quit My Job

#23 Learn to Salsa

#24 Fall in Love

#1 LEARN POLE DANCING

ONE

I ran my fingertips over the well-worn piece of notebook paper. It had permanent fold lines from being hidden and re-hidden like a secret I wasn't brave enough to keep out in the open. I'd written the list at a time when I didn't really believe I'd ever accomplish anything on it.

And yet—here I was.

Which meant it was time to look at the first item.

I rolled over on my bed and stared down at it. When I had added it to my list, it was just a fun little whim, not something I thought I would actually do. But then again, I never would have thought I'd be able to lose so much weight either.

"What was I thinking?" I gnawed on the pencil between my teeth. I was tempted to just erase the item and replace it with something else. No one would have to know.

But *I* would know.

I cringed at the idea of actually following through with it. But I had to do it. I had to. It was on the list.

I groaned and rolled over on my bed. I stared up at the

cracks in my ceiling for a moment. Then I sat up with a new determination.

"Yes, I will do this," I said, looking down at the item on the list. "Pole dancing class, here I come." I was attempting to sound brave for myself, when I caught sight of the time on my alarm clock.

I grabbed my jeans from the laundry basket and slid them up over my hips with my eyes squeezed shut—because optimism is powerful, but denim is stronger.

When the zipper went up in one smooth, glorious motion, I nearly applauded.

I smiled at my reflection in the tall mirror as I studied the way that my jeans hugged my hips and rear. All my hard work, all the passed-up snacks—had really paid off.

My body looked different and I *felt* different.

"Hey, you sexy lady," I said to the shapely woman in the mirror, twisting my hips first one way and then the other. "Do you come here often?" I asked in the deepest voice I could muster and batted my long lashes at my own reflection.

"Uh, Sammy?" a voice said from the doorway of my bedroom.

I froze and held my breath for another reason.

It was Max.

Max, my best friend.

Max, with the deep green eyes and a body that would make any woman glance in his direction.

I turned around slowly to face him, not wanting him to see what I knew would be sheer embarrassment on my face.

"What?" I asked as innocently as I could.

He stared at me with one quirked eyebrow, looking as

sexy as ever. Max was not conventionally handsome, but a quirky kind of cute, like the kind of guy that got the lead in romantic movies. Not drop-dead gorgeous, but just goofy enough to grow on you and make you think he was adorable by the end of the movie.

"I've heard of bisexual, but what would you call it if you try to pick yourself up?" He smiled and leaned against the doorway.

God, but that smile made me want to snuggle right up to him.

Friend, I reminded myself. Max, my friend.

No matter what my fantasies wanted to believe, we had never been anything more than that. Of course, when my eyes were closed late at night he played a very active role in my life.

"I don't discriminate, Max. If I see something as hot and lovely as the lady in the mirror happens to be, I've got to give it a shot." I grinned, hoping he would not notice that I was mortified.

"Well, I'd have to agree with you there," he said with a laugh and shook his head as he walked into my room.

We had spent hours sitting on this very bed on several occasions. Him thinking we were just watching a movie and me praying he would lean over and kiss me.

He never did. At least, not in reality.

But the things that he had done in my mind...

"What are you up to today?" he asked, perched on the end of my bed.

"I'm going out," I said, fluffing my newly bleached blonde hair with my fingers.

He was smiling as he watched me.

"Are you going out to break some man's heart?" he asked, brushing his thick dark hair away from his eyes.

He was studying me intently. It always unnerved me when he looked at me so closely. I could never tell if it was with approval, desire, or confusion.

"Sure, of course." I stuck my tongue out at him.

He tilted his head to the side. "So you *don't* have a date?"

"Stop it, Max." I shook my head as I turned away from him. Only then did I spot the black leotard and tights still lying on the bed. I felt a rush of horror flood me.

If Max saw them, he'd be full of questions that I didn't want to answer.

"Stop what?" He leaned back on the bed. His hand came to rest just beside the tights. "I'm just curious. You haven't had a date in a while."

"Thanks for pointing that out." I reached past him to nudge the leotard away from where he was sitting. Sometimes having a man for a best friend was not ideal. "I've had plenty of dates. You don't know everything there is to know about me."

Of course I hadn't had *any* dates lately, but Max didn't need to know that. As confident as I was in my beauty, it would appear that being big and beautiful hadn't translated to a man tripping head-over-heels in love with me—not yet anyways—a fact that was beginning to make me slightly nervous. At thirty-two, my clock wasn't quite ticking just yet, but I did feel that I was ready to fall in love.

"Then tell me," Max said, jolting me out of my thoughts. "Are you keeping secrets from me?"

"Secrets?" I laughed a little at the idea.

In the fourteen years that Max and I had been friends I had never been able to keep a secret from him. But this time I was determined to do it. My dignity depended on it.

I sat down on the bed next to him and slid my hand casually back across the bedspread toward the tights and leotard, now behind him on the bed.

"So are you saving yourself for me, is that it?" he asked and met my eyes.

TWO

With Max sitting so close, I could feel the heat of the outside of his thigh pressed against my jeans. I tried to keep my breathing steady as I looked into his eyes.

I knew that he was joking. I'd seen the women he dated, and they did *not* look like me. But he was always lavishing me with praise, as if I was just as beautiful. Sometimes, I wasn't sure if he was teasing me or being serious, but he never put me down.

"I'm going to a class," I said quietly, snatching up my black leotard and tights.

"What kind of class?" He leaned back on my bed, placing his hands behind him.

"Sort of a dance class," I said, thankful that I'd gotten the leotard out of the way before he could spot it.

"What's this?" Max sat up with a piece of paper in his hand.

I thought nothing of it at first, until I realized what it was.

"Max, give me that!"

My heart was pounding. I so did not want to deal with telling him about this right now. But he was already reading it.

"Pole dancing," he read out loud. "Why is this highlighted and surrounded by stars?" He glanced up at me as I lunged across the bed, grabbing the list out of his hand.

"Mine!" I said just a little too loudly, and he laughed.

"Is that the dance class? Pole dancing?" He narrowed his eyes as he looked at me.

"Maybe," I said, tucking the list into my pocket.

"So that's what the leotard is for." He had a mischievous grin on his face, and I was annoyed that he'd seen the outfit despite my best efforts to get it out of his eyesight. "Put it on. Let me see you in it."

"No way, Max." And he was not going to convince me otherwise. "Some things are private."

He was quiet for a few seconds as he looked at me intently. "Even from me?"

Oh, definitely from you.

"This has nothing to do with you, so wipe that pout off your face. It's not happening." I got up from the bed, leotard in hand. "The only people that are going to see me in this are the teacher and the other students in the class."

"Well, where can I sign up?"

I laughed and threw my leotard at him. "Only if you try this on first."

He grinned and shook his head. "Not my style, Sammy. But I think you'll look fantastic in it. I dare you to wear just that to class. Don't cover yourself up so much."

"I know, I know, I've lost so much weight, I should be

proud, blah, blah, blah," I said, walking across the room towards the mirror.

I *had* lost about seventy pounds over the past year, leaving me at my new svelte size of one hundred and eighty pounds.

"No, Sammy," he said and sat forward a bit on the bed. "You should be proud no matter what you weigh, because you're gorgeous. Nothing can change that."

I smiled at him in the mirror and he smiled back. He always knew just what to say to make me feel better.

"So are you going to do it?" he asked, his smile turning devilish. "Just the tights and the leotard, nothing else."

"Maybe. But you won't find out because you're not going!"

"Fine." He threw himself backwards on my bed, silent for several seconds.

I wondered what he was thinking, as there was nothing particularly interesting about the ceiling that he seemed to be studying so intently.

"So what's the paper for?" he asked. "I noticed it's like a list."

"None of your business," I said, turning back to the mirror, trying to look as casual as possible.

"So many secrets." He frowned and stared at my reflection. "I thought I was your best friend."

Max was very good at laying on the guilt, but I didn't have time for any of it at the moment.

"Best *guy* friend." I smiled at him. "That means you don't get to be in on *some* secrets. You should be grateful for that," I added with a laugh.

"I'm not grateful at all. That's just discrimination," he said, and I couldn't help but notice that he seemed genuinely upset. "I thought you were more evolved than that."

"Nope, I'm not more evolved than that." I turned to face him. "Now get off my bed, get out of my apartment, and go fix some computers."

He wiped his hand over his eyes and mouth and shook his head. "That is *not* what I do."

I knew what was coming next and I really didn't have time for it.

"Would you like me to explain it again?"

"No, please don't." I laughed and shook my head.

Max had tried several times to explain his high-tech job to me, but I still didn't quite get it.

"I think you should quit your tinkering and come back to the Fluff and Stuff."

"Ah, the good old Fluff and Stuff," Max said with a slight shake of his head. "The only laundromat where I can wash my boxers and buy a box of junk."

"Like you wear boxers." I winked at him.

It was Max's turn to blush a little.

"And it's not junk, it's unique one-of-a-kind items." I was always quick to defend the job that had come to mean a lot to me over the years. "I love the Fluff and Stuff. You used to love it too."

"Right, while I was still in college, studying for my *real* job."

His words stung a little and took me by surprise. I frowned as I turned away from him.

"It's real enough to me," I said quietly.

"I'm sorry, Sam. I didn't mean it that way," he said quickly. "I just meant—you know—when we started working there, we were both just out of high school. It was a college gig for both of us."

"But you finished college and I couldn't pick a major." I shook my head, annoyed at where the conversation was headed. I started to push Max towards the door. "I have to get to class."

Max turned to face me. "You know I didn't mean anything by it."

I looked back at him and couldn't help but smile. His obvious concern for my feelings *was* touching.

"I know you didn't. Besides, I'm the manager now, and that's much more important than fixing computers," I said with a shrug.

"That is *not* what I do."

"Well, whatever you do"—I waved my hand towards the door—"go do it, so I can get ready for class."

"Remember—just the leotard!" he hollered over his shoulder, and I could hear him laughing as he walked away.

THREE

I waited until I heard the door close and then checked to be sure he was gone.

As soon as it was safe, I jumped onto the bed where he had been lying, pretending he was still there next to me.

"Oh, Max, I'll wear anything for you," I said in my sexiest voice patting the bed beside me lightly. I snuggled a pillow close, pretending it was Max I was hugging.

Bang! I jumped when I heard a loud sound against the window by my bed.

I looked up to see Max's face on the other side of the glass.

"Just the leotard!" he said, laughing as he turned to walk away.

I groaned and pushed my face into the pillow, hoping he hadn't seen me acting so strange. I really needed to curb my silliness if I had any hopes of landing Max—or any man, for that matter.

As I lay there, I thought about what he'd said. He did

have a valid point, actually. I had a right to walk around town in my leotard if I felt like it. I should be proud of my body, in all of its beauty.

The more I thought it through, I started to think that maybe not covering myself up would be a good way to reinforce my confidence.

That was a big part of what the list was all about. It was a bucket list of sorts that I'd started when I was at a heavier weight. It was a list of all the things I wanted to do when I was thinner *and* feeling more confident about myself.

The first big change I'd made hadn't been officially on the list, but when I entered "onederland"—with a weigh-in that week of one hundred ninety-eight pounds—I knew that I had to celebrate by doing something big.

I'd been thinking of bleaching my mousy brown hair for years, never quite sure that I could pull it off. That very next weekend, I came out of the salon feeling like a new woman—a blonde who was ready to start having way more fun than I'd been having.

So far, a few months later, I was still waiting for the fun factor to *really* kick in, but I didn't regret my new look, and it helped me to realize that I didn't need to wait to achieve some fantastic goal number before I started attacking some of these list items. I was ready to start living my new life—parts of which were now written down on the list—sooner rather than later.

The first *official* item on my bucket list was learning to pole dance, which was what led me to the leotard and tights in the first place. I thought there was nothing more seductive than a woman who could move and shake her body in just the right way, so I'd called a local gym and signed up for the class that I'd seen advertised. No questions asked, not giving myself a chance—so far—to back out.

I shed my jeans—noticing again how much easier they were to take on and off these days—and pulled on my tights, followed by the leotard. The tights were sheer and just a little thicker than pantyhose. The leotard was solid black. I had considered the one with the sparkles, but I didn't want to come across as too flashy on my first day—or too much like a third grader. I smiled, already recognizing that I just *was* a bit silly—no use denying it.

I left my apartment knowing deep down that there would be a lot more happening at this class than just learning to dance.

I did not, in fact, cover myself up, and with one last deep breath, I set out down the sidewalk proudly with my head held high. I was taking back my power as a sexy, beautiful woman. I was demonstrating that I could be comfortable and happy with my body, and this pole dancing class was going to count for my daily exercise too.

So check and check.

Confidence and cardio. What more could a girl want?

Outside, it was a bit colder than I'd expected. As I walked down the sidewalk, I crossed my arms over my chest just in case the new sports bra I'd gotten on sale wasn't carrying its end of the bargain. No need to give the neighbors a show.

I'd already offended my neighbor next door just this week with my lack of knowledge about anything related to social media. How was I supposed to know that it was rude to write notes to her on her Facebook wall?

As I walked, I noticed how *unnoticed* I was. Which was comforting for about five seconds. Then it became deeply offensive. Here I was, a fairly attractive woman, walking down the block in just a leotard and tights, and no one even glanced in my direction. Everyone appeared too busy to even bother to notice a nearly naked crazy lady—well, I wasn't exactly crazy, but they didn't know this.

I tried not to be offended, but really, the way I was dressed deserved a second glance.

"Would you like a sample?"

A tray was shoved directly in front of me as I was walking along the sidewalk.

I stared down at the assortment of bakery treats. There were small brownies, cookies, and what looked like a tiny slice of chocolate mousse cake.

"No, thank you."

I continued walking forward slowly as I looked up at the man holding the tray. My heart skipped a beat. He was handsome in a very conventional way.

"It's free," he said, seemingly determined to tempt me further.

"No, I shouldn't," I said quickly and tried to step around him. He was wearing an apron that displayed a nearby bakery's name. I knew he was only doing his job, but waving that brownie in my face was downright cruel.

Of course I could always just duck into the bakery for a bit instead of going to the class. No one would ever know.

I shook my head. *I* would know.

"No, thank you. I'm on my way to a class," I said, while trying to move around the man.

For some odd reason he stepped at the same time as I did and in the same direction. I caught my foot on his foot and we both began to stumble. I grabbed his arm to try to steady myself, and in doing so, tipped the tray of bakery items. I got my footing, but the pastries went flying.

"Oh no, I'm so sorry," I said quickly. "I'm just in a rush to get to this pole dancing class—"

As soon as the words were out of my mouth I realized what I'd said. I had just told this perfect stranger, who was trying to force-feed me brownies, that I was rushing off to dance on a pole.

He looked up at me with a sly smile as he collected the sweets that had fallen to the ground. "Well, you wouldn't want to be late for that, would you?" He grinned.

I stared down at him, perplexed. I wasn't sure if he was teasing me or agreeing with me. Either way, I had a class to get to. I had "just said no" to the brownies and I was proud of myself for that.

As I hurried the rest of the way to the class, I tried not to think of Max, brownies, or anything that made me feel less than sexy and capable.

I reached the small building and stopped just outside the door, taking a few deep breaths. Only then did I see the smattering of crumbs all over my leotard. I brushed them off, thankful that I'd noticed them before entering the gym.

I took one last deep breath as I reached for the handle on the door, trying my best to remain calm.

FOUR

I am sexy. I am beautiful. I am comfortable in my skin, and I am proud of my body. This was the mantra that I was chanting in my head as I walked into my first pole dancing class.

When I'd been getting up the courage to sign up for the class, I'd told myself that there'd be other women my shape and size there too. After I walked into the room, I could see that this was not the case. *At all.* It was a bit hard to tell the pole from the pole dancers. They were all equally vertical and intimidating.

"Welcome," a shrill voice called from the small reception desk set up in the corner of the open gym.

"I think I might be in the wrong place." I hesitated.

The women were looking at me with funny expressions on their faces.

I started to turn back toward the door, but stopped when I saw the teacher walking toward me.

He couldn't have been more than five foot three, which was several inches shorter than me. He wore a black leotard with a pink ribbon wrapped around the middle and a matching pink sweatband to hold back his perfectly trimmed brown curls. His smile was so wide that it seemed to take up his whole face. He was friendly in a way that I couldn't ignore.

"Oh no, you're right where you're supposed to be. I'm Randy," he said as he reached out to grab my hand. "Come in, come in. I'll introduce you to the ladies."

I gritted my teeth. The last thing I wanted to do was meet the ladies.

"Ladies, this is—" He paused and looked in my direction.

"Samantha—Sammy—Bradford." I stumbled over my own name. It wasn't that I was feeling insecure—it just wasn't exactly what I'd expected. I loved my body, but It looked a little more sausagey than saucy when compared to these women.

Less femme fatale. More deli counter.

Randy smiled at me. "Sammy, this is Mia, Mara, Melody, and Janice, my star students," he smiled proudly.

I eyed Janice closely. She must be the black sheep.

"Now, these ladies have had a few weeks of training already, Samantha, so please understand that no one expects you to be able to do what they can do, okay?" Randy said as he walked back to the front of the group.

I nodded and settled down on the floor near Janice. The black sheep were always the best ones to sidle up to, in my experience. I hoped that she would help me break the ice so that I could begin to feel a bit more comfortable around the group.

"Mara, why don't you show us what we learned last week?" Randy said and stepped back to watch.

"Gladly," Mara said and lifted her chin.

I could see why. Her chin was perfect. Not too pointy, not too round, and there was only one of them.

Mara stood up, showing off her five-foot-nine, too-skinny-to-get-on-a-scale body, and wrapped her arms around the pole.

Randy hit a button on the remote he had tucked into his pink ribbon, and the lights dimmed. Music began to play with a steady rhythmic thump. A bright light clicked on and shone right on the stripper pole that Mara was clinging to.

She began to gyrate her hips up against the pole as she worked her way a few feet up off the ground.

I stared at her as she moved, graceful as any dancer I'd ever seen. Her long dark hair tumbled down like a waterfall when she tipped her head back and smiled at the rest of us.

Perfect, I thought. Not a word I would use to describe what I anticipated doing on the stage.

"Brilliant," Randy said and waved her away dismissively. "Now, let's see what Samantha has to show us. Mrow!" He feigned a cat's paw with his hand and swiped it at me.

Seriously? He had gone from charismatically friendly to disturbingly cheesy.

I reminded myself about the list. I had come this far. I wasn't going to quit now. This didn't seem like your typical class, but I was willing to give it a shot.

I stepped to the front of the room, feeling nervous despite

the little pep talk I'd just given myself. I turned to face the other women, knowing that they had their critical gazes focused on me.

"Okay, now keep in mind that this is my first time, ladies," I said, looking around the room, willing them to cut me a small break as I prepared to give it a good try. None of them were overly friendly, but Janice managed a small smile in my direction. "Here I go!" I plastered a big smile on my face and grabbed the pole, spinning myself around it as hard as I could.

I lost my grip during the very first spin and went sailing off the edge of the platform. I would have been mortified with just that, but no, I had to go ahead and commit a total face-plant on the gym floor.

"Oh, no. Are you okay? We don't really have insurance for this," Randy said, sounding nervous as he helped me up.

"I'm fine," I squeaked out, smoothing my leotard as I tried to catch my breath and calm myself. How was I supposed to know that the pole would be so darn slippery?

"Try again." Randy was quick to encourage me, and he seemed to be telling me with his steady eye contact to ignore the other women's barely restrained laughter.

"I don't know if I can," I said, already sweaty and feeling my face grow warm under what I was sure was a nice shade of red. I couldn't believe I had ever written this activity down on my list.

He leaned close to me and whispered in my ear. "You need to teach these skinny girls what sexy is, Samantha. You use that beautiful body, you seduce us with those curves—

you get up there and show them what it means to be a woman."

His words sunk in and I felt my heart pumping. He was right. Voluptuous—that was what I called myself. I had the sweet figure that men liked, no matter what other women might say. This was *my* time to prove to myself how sexy I was. This was *my* bucket list, not theirs!

FIVE

I marched back up on to the platform. I wiped my hands on my leotard and then grabbed the pole. Randy turned the music up and added a strobe-light effect. I imagined my name being announced to an adoring crowd of seedy men who had nothing better to do than spend their paychecks on half-dressed women humping poles, and I was quite proud of myself.

I could feel thc music pumping through my body right along with the movement of my muscles. Everything became vivid. I could sense the pole against my palm, as if it was the only thing that mattered. I could feel the brush of air across my sweat-covered skin. I could smell the chemicals in the rubber mats on the floor and the strange cologne that the teacher was wearing. But more than anything, I could feel my body—alive, powerful, unapologetic.

For once, it wasn't something to hide. It was something to use.

I leaned so far back that my hair brushed the platform, and then slowly pulled myself back up. I hooked my leg around the pole and tried to shimmy up it a bit, before sliding back down. I didn't get too far, but it didn't matter; the music was still flowing through me. I spun around the pole, this time careful to keep my grip. My hair flew in my face, but I just blew it away with a sexy huff.

I was so caught up in the dance that I didn't hear Randy. It wasn't until he cut off the music and the lights came back on that I realized I should stop. The women seated around the platform were staring up at me with their mouths open.

Randy had both eyebrows raised. "Well, Ms. Samantha, I think you were hiding a talent." He laughed and clapped his hands loudly. "Maybe next class you'll save some time for the others, though."

"Time?" I asked with surprise as I looked around.

"You've been dancing for twenty minutes!" Janice said. "How did you do that thing you did?" She genuinely sounded awestruck.

"What thing?" I was very confused. How did I lose twenty minutes? I had just let my body move to the music. Had I done anything embarrassing?

"That thing where you had one leg over your head and the other one was spread way out—" Janice tried to demonstrate.

I stared at the woman and what she was attempting to do with her legs.

"Oh, no way, I did not do that," I said firmly. Just looking at Janice contorting herself in such a way made me want to snuggle down on a nice soft sofa.

"Oh, yes, you did." Randy grinned. "You have a sexy beast in you, Sammy, and you let it out on that pole today!"

I blinked.

Sexy beast? I had been aiming for mildly competent mammal.

I was stunned as I wiped some sweat from my forehead. Was it possible I had just not realized what I was doing?

"I want you to teach me," Mara said as she looked up at me with wide eyes. "Please, will you?"

I laughed and shook my head. "I have no idea what I did. I just let the music flow through me. I just moved to the beat."

"It was amazing," the other women chimed in, all applauding my efforts.

Mara frowned as she glanced at me and then at her own figure. "I wish I had hips that could do that."

"All hips can do that," I said with confidence. "We just have to find a way to let our bodies be free."

"Maybe we should all just get naked," Janice said.

"Janice!" Mara gasped and stared at her friend.

"I was just kidding!" Janice said, looking only slightly embarrassed.

I had to laugh a little. But I didn't think Janice was that far off. I felt amazing. I knew Max's insistence that I not cover up my body had given me a chance to shake off my stage fright. Of course, I had no idea what I had just done or why the ladies had admired me so much, but it didn't matter. It had given me the ego boost I needed to feel wonderful about myself.

I strutted down the sidewalk in my leotard and tights, not caring who saw me. I now knew what power my body held. In fact, I must have still been exuding some seductive energy, because men on the street began whistling and hollering at me. I usually frowned on this type of behavior, but this time it was nice. I winked back at them. I even waved to one. I felt like a movie star.

Then I realized that it wasn't just the men staring at me. It was, in fact, everyone I passed on the sidewalk and even people across the street. Cars were honking their horns as they drove by. Only then did I realize I should not be feeling a cool breeze against my—

Oh no.

Oh no, no, no.

"Oh my god!" I grabbed the backside of my leotard. It had split right down the middle, and I was walking down the street with my rear bare for everyone to see. I held the material together and ran for the nearest doorway.

"No, no, no." I ducked into the building without even bothering to look to see what it was. A group of people were sitting around in a small circle on folding chairs. Most of them had cups of coffee in their hands.

"Pardon me," I said as I tried to keep my rear facing away from them. "Would you have a restroom?" I said a silent prayer in my head while I waited for a reply.

"Are you here for the meeting?" a woman in the middle of the group asked.

"Meeting?"

"SA," one of the men in the circle piped up.

"SA?" I was still confused. "Uh, sure."

"Okay, hurry up, we've already started," the woman said, pointing out the bathroom.

SIX

I ducked right in to the restroom and locked the door behind me.

Once inside, I breathed a sigh of relief. When I opened my eyes I was startled by the posters on the wall.

When sex is a have-to instead of a pleasure, it's addiction, one poster declared, with the picture of a man looking desperate sitting on the edge of a bed.

Do you have multiple partners in one night? Have you ever blacked out and not realized that you've had a sexual encounter? Then you might be a sex addict, another poster explained.

"SA," I said in a whisper. "Sex addicts—oh my god!"

I had officially pole-danced my way into the wrong support group.

I groaned and peeked over my shoulder at my fully bare bottom. The more I tried to tug the material together, the more it frayed apart. The only thing between my bottom and the rest of the world was a thin pair of black pantyhose, and that appeared to have a big hole starting as well. This was not going to be good.

I looked around for something—anything—to use to disguise my backside. I grabbed for some paper towels, thinking I could make a little skirt out of them, but when I pulled the first one out, it was also the last one.

"Hello. Are you coming out of there?" a voice called out from the other side of the door. "Other people have to use the bathroom, you know!"

I looked in the mirror and remembered the pep talk I'd given myself earlier. I took a deep breath and knew that I just had to get home and put some pants on. I placed the paper towel over my bottom and opened the door to the bathroom. I held my chin up high and marched right out.

"Uh, miss?" one of the men said as he watched me walk past, my paper towel flapping in the breeze from the spinning ceiling fans.

"Nothing to see here..." I walked fast across the room and opened the door. As it fell shut behind me, I heard the woman whisper to the other people in the circle.

"Some of us just aren't ready to ask for help yet. One day she'll admit she has a problem and we'll be here for her."

I groaned and tried to edge my way along the wall. I didn't think I was going to make it all the way back to my apartment like this. Would I be arrested for indecent exposure? Would I offend nuns and small children? My heart was pounding with embarrassment. I was certain that I could not possibly feel worse.

Then a car driving beside me began to slow down. I pretended not to notice.

Just keep going.

"Sam, is that you?" a familiar voice asked as the car pulled to a stop.

In that moment, I cursed myself for challenging the universe. I had been certain nothing could make my situation worse, and now I was about to be proved wrong. Not only was I to be humiliated in front of my entire neighborhood, but also in front of the man whose face occupied ninety percent of my fantasies.

I refused to look in his direction.

"Go away, Max!" I said, already too embarrassed for words.

"Oh, come on, what's wrong?" he asked.

I knew he wasn't going to let it go unless I confessed.

I glanced up and over at him. Again, things got worse. He was the passenger in a flashy convertible, with a drop-dead gorgeous woman, and I was walking around with a paper towel covering my bottom. Ha ha, universe.

"Nothing. I'm fine." I kept walking. I might have been able to ask for a ride, but I couldn't bring myself to do it. I would rather walk home in shame than reveal what had happened to me to Max.

He climbed out of the car and followed after me.

"Max?" the woman who was driving called out, not sounding happy at all.

Max ignored her as he caught up with me. "Why do you have that paper towel—"

The woman in the convertible—apparently annoyed that Max would abandon her—drove off, causing a slight breeze to ruffle my paper towel.

"Oh my god." Max ran up behind me and put his hands on my waist, using his own body to shield me from view. "What happened?" He was laughing, seemingly unconcerned about his fleeing ride.

"It's not funny," I said, feeling increasingly more irritated. I tried not to think about how close he was to me.

"Oh, yes it is." He laughed harder and had to rest his head on the back of my neck to keep from losing his balance, he was laughing so hard.

"I'm so very glad that my embarrassing moment is amusing to you," I said, putting some distance between us as I turned around to look at him. "Now, give me your shirt."

"My shirt?" He looked down at it. "No way, this is brand new. Besides, I don't want to walk around with no shirt on." He glanced around. "People have no decency any more."

I glared over my shoulder at him and pointed to the paper towel.

"If you make me walk home like this, I promise you I will turn all of your underwear pink."

I had been doing most of his laundry, whenever I did my own, for the past ten years.

"Well, what are you going to give me for it?"

He was being so obnoxious.

"My undying affection," I said as sweetly as I could.

Our conversation was starting to draw more attention. The paper towel was steadily flapping in the light breeze.

"I already have that, don't I?" The expression on his face changed a little bit.

For just a moment I thought he might be hinting that he knew about my crush.

"Okay, fine, then what do you want?"

I was getting impatient now. I didn't like that he was being so cruel when I was so embarrassed. He knew he could get me to do just about anything, and he was taking advantage of it.

SEVEN

There was a strange expression on Max's face again, but only for a second. "If I give you my shirt, then you have to promise me you'll let me read that piece of paper—that list of yours," he said with a smile.

"That's private." I was seriously annoyed now. "Absolutely not—no deal," I said, walking away.

Max reached out and snatched the paper towel from my hand. When I felt it go, I gasped.

"Max!" I screamed and backed right into him to cover myself up. He slid a hand around my waist, holding me securely against him, and whispered beside my ear.

"The list, Sam, or you get to walk the next three blocks au naturel." He laughed and all at once I realized that he meant it. He was playing with me, but it was a side of Max that I wasn't used to.

"Fine."

"Yes!" He pumped his fist in a gesture of victory.

I glared at him as he removed his shirt with care. He was

still standing behind me when he slid it between us and then reached around to tie the sleeves in a loose knot. Every brush of his skin, every accidental touch was thrilling for me, even though I was also feeling quite angry with him.

The rush of emotion was confusing.

"Better?" he murmured.

I turned around to face him and found that he was still grinning. The unexpected scent of the cologne from his shirt, now tied around me, and seeing him standing there bare-chested, was making me feel quite giddy. I tried to regain my composure.

"You forget you ever saw that," I said, shoving a finger towards his face. "One word about this and you will pay for it."

"I can't possibly forget it," he said, teasing me. "It's burned into my mind." He laughed.

I laughed too, but I wasn't sure if he was joking. Had he found my naked rear that unattractive? Knowing the types of women he usually dated, I figured it was possible.

"Sorry about your ride," I said. "I don't think she appreciated the view."

"Oh—Bianca." He rolled his eyes and tilted his head to the side. "Oh, please, Max, just help me pick this red lipstick, or this red lipstick? Which one?" he said in a high-pitched voice.

"Oh, she can't be *that* bad."

I *wanted* her to be that bad. I wanted her to be vapid and intolerable. I wanted her to be anything but what Max wanted in a woman.

"She's worse." He squeezed his eyes shut tight for a

moment. "I don't know if it was the car or her big brown eyes, but something convinced me to give it a shot, and let me tell you, I would have rather been pole dancing." He met my eyes. "Unfortunately, *I* wasn't invited."

I couldn't help but smile at his words. It seemed as if he really did want to spend time with me. As friends, I reminded myself. But I had to wonder, just for a moment: was Bianca meant to make me jealous?

Max placed his arm around my shoulders. "So tell me about the class. Did you fall in love with the pole?" he asked as he fell into step beside me and we walked back toward my apartment. "Obviously, you had a bit of fun," he said, grinning. "Did that happen before or after the class?"

"After!" I glared at him. "Yes, I had a little *too* much fun." I laughed now, thinking about the class. "It was good. I was actually very good at it." I was feeling proud of myself again as I remembered.

"Great, so when Fluff and Stuff goes under, you have a new career waiting for you." He ducked just in time, before my hand could connect with the side of his head.

He did know me far too well, and just how to get under my skin.

"It's not going under," I said with pride. "Not with me at its helm."

"Okay, if you say so." He shook his head. "Just remember, I warned you."

"How could I forget?" I asked with a slight roll of my eyes. He often told me I should find a new job, but there was something about the whirr of the washing machines and the scent of the hot dogs that felt like home to me. I had worked there for so long that it was a huge part of my life.

"Just because you gave up on Fluff and Stuff doesn't mean I ever will."

"I didn't give up on it, Sammy. I grew up."

His harsh words cut me to the bone.

"Too bad for you," I shot back.

He glanced over at me and squeezed my shoulder. "Good thing I have you around to keep me young."

"Is that all I'm good for?" I asked as we reached my apartment.

He turned slowly to look at me.

When his eyes met mine, I felt it—that spark—that tingling of every muscle in my body. His lips were so close, his eyes so filled with what I wanted to believe was desire. It would take the absolute smallest effort to simply lean forward and kiss him.

"That and grilled cheese." He laughed, sliding his arm off my shoulder to open the door.

He had a key. I made a mental note to change that.

As I stepped into my apartment, he started to follow me inside.

"I think I've had enough excitement for one day and no, I'm not making grilled cheese." I walked over to grab the blanket thrown over the end of the sofa, wrapping it around my body in relief. "I'd like to hide under my covers now and forget about mooning the entire neighborhood."

Max smiled, looking mischievous again. "But we had a deal, remember?"

"A deal?" I asked, a little confused. Then it hit me. The list!

EIGHT

I thought about the things I had written on my bucket list so far, and most importantly, the one item written in big bold letters at the very bottom. "Be with Max".

"Uh, sure," I said as we walked into the living room. "But wait out here, because I need to change." I pushed him down on the sofa.

He grabbed the remote and began flipping through the channels as I hurried into the bedroom. I threw my jeans back on over my torn leotard and then reached for the list. I snatched up another piece of paper and began scrawling random ideas on it. It shouldn't have taken me much more than a few minutes, but then I began obsessing. What would Max find interesting?

Study computer science, I scribbled down. Then I frowned. I didn't think he was going to believe that one for a minute. I crumpled up the piece of paper and grabbed a new one. I started writing everything that came to mind.

Skinny-dipping

Parasailing

Eggs

Cheese

"Focus, Sammy," I muttered. "We are not manifesting omelets.". I crumpled up that piece of paper too.

On the third attempt, I just wrote down everything I had seen in movies.

Sail a boat across the sea

Design a new piece of clothing

Find the perfect shell

Skip a rock

I stretched it out to about twenty items and hoped that he'd buy it. Then I tucked the real list safely away. I was just about to take it out to him when I remembered what he'd already seen. I added pole dancing to the top and highlighted it with my marker. I hurried out into the living room, where Max was waiting for me.

When I handed him the list, he cackled in an evil-sounding voice, but then his amusement faded as he looked it over.

"Hm, see if I share my shirt with you next time." He frowned.

"What? Why?" I said. Coming up with that list had been a lot of work.

"There are no stars around it," he said. "The list I saw had stars on it."

I sank down on the sofa and glanced over at him.

"I get it," he said, sounding a bit sad. "I know how this will work. You want romance, so soon you'll land a guy and then good old Max will just be a memory."

I was confused for a minute, but then I remembered that several of the items I'd jotted down towards the end of my fake list had to do with dating and meeting "Mr. Right".

I studied him closely. It was always hard to tell when he was joking.

"Max, you are always going to be part of my life," I said with conviction. "I can't possibly live without you."

He sighed, folding his arms across his still-bare chest.

I laid my head across his lap and looked up at him, pouting my lips. "Don't be mad," I said as I gazed up into his eyes, trying hard to bat my eyelashes at him in a teasing way.

He stared down at me for a long moment. "How can I be with that face?" He laughed, his sense of humor returning in full force. "So, no list, I guess?"

"You can have your shirt back." I offered it to him with a wide smile.

"No, keep it," he chuckled. "Never know when you might have another wardrobe malfunction."

As Max left the apartment, I knew he was still a little bit annoyed. He had this thing about trust. I couldn't exactly figure him out, even though we'd been friends for so long.

He dated a lot of women, but never for long. He was willing to be intimate—hugging and snuggling—but he never shared too much about himself. He fascinated me.

One minute I would be completely convinced that he was as into me as I was into him, but then he would hook up with someone like Bianca, or give no other signs, and I'd be left feeling sure that I was making it all up in my head.

I plopped down on my bed and closed my eyes.

Instantly, Max without his shirt popped into my mind. I sighed and tried to replace his face with that of someone else. But it didn't work. I sat up and wiped at my eyes. I knew that as long as I was alone in my apartment, I was going to be obsessing about him. I needed to get my mind on something else.

The best way to do that was to go to work. It wasn't my shift, but I didn't mind. I needed an excuse to escape my memories of the day.

The shop was only a few blocks away from my apartment. As I walked, I kept a close eye out for any of the men who had been catcalling me earlier. Now that my pants actually covered my rear end, I didn't seem to get as much attention.

As I neared the shop, I smiled at the sign. It was made in the shape of a big bubble. Fluff and Stuff. It was a simple concept: people get bored while doing their laundry; having a shop to browse through is entertaining. But when I envisioned it, I saw it as much more than that. I had dreams of open mic nights and a community garden.

As Max liked to say, I had nothing *but* dreams.

When I stepped inside the shop I spotted Claudia nearly asleep on the counter.

"Tough night?" I asked as I walked up to her.

"You have no idea." She groaned and sat up.

She was right. I didn't have any idea what it was like to have a screaming, drooling, pooping, unsatisfiable infant keeping me up all night.

"Why don't you go home?" I said. "I have nothing to do

I was about to open it up, when I realized something was missing.

I walked across the room to dim the lights a little. I didn't want anything glaring on the screen. When I sat back down again, I realized that something *else* was missing.

I crossed the room to turn on some soft music.

Perfect. I settled back down on the couch.

Now, what should I write about?

Should I be witty? Should I be dramatic? What should the first word be?

My mind was spinning with ideas. I could write about the bucket list, but I wasn't sure I wanted that to be my first post. I could write about my weight loss journey, but I was afraid that would make readers believe that was all the blog was about. I needed something... I could always write about Max.

No, no, no. I reminded myself that I was trying to stop thinking—obsessing—over Max.

I needed something else to keep me focused.

"Cinnamon," I said out loud. "Cinnamon will give me that intelligent vibe that I'm needing in here."

I walked across the room to grab the candle from the shelf in the kitchen and carried it into the living room, setting it in the middle of the coffee table. "Perfect." I started to sit back down and then realized that I needed to actually light the candle—which meant that I had to find matches or a lighter.

Looking around the living room, I tried to remember what I might have done with a lighter. I knew I'd had one for my last birthday cake, but I hadn't seen it since.

I rummaged through the drawers in the kitchen. Then I

the rest of the day, so I thought I'd hang out here. No need for both of us to be here."

"Oh, thanks," Claudia said with relief. "There's a few loads running, but it's been pretty slow."

I nodded. "Go get some rest."

NINE

Claudia walked out of the shop, looking like she was in desperate need of a nap.

I watched her go. She was only in her early twenties and was already married. Sometimes I was jealous of her. Not because of how she looked, or her husband, but because she had moved on in life, checking off each milestone, while I had remained generally the same.

It was starting to really sink in with me that things were changing—that time was passing me by. Just like in college, when I couldn't decide on a major, I still had no real idea what I wanted out of life—*except for that tasty caramel crunch candy bar we just started selling in the shop.*

My mind wandered and so did I as I walked over to the candy bars, fully intending to rip one open and settle up with the register later. But just as my fingers curled around the forbidden snack, I recalled how good it felt to fit into my jeans earlier today.

"No," I said, feeling committed. "I'm not going to let a little incident throw off my entire journey."

I released the candy bar and walked away like a hero in a slow-motion commercial for self-restraint.

No dramatic music played. But it should have.

One of the dryers buzzed.

I popped it open to find the load still a little damp. I set it to spin again and sat down in a bucket-style plastic chair to watch it. The swirl of the dryer was oddly soothing to me. I wasn't sure why. Perhaps because I had spent so many years watching it. No matter what the reason, it always seemed to help me clear my mind.

After the way that Max had spoken to me, I needed some mind clearing. In fact, I wished I could toss my brain into a spin cycle. But no matter what I did, I knew I wouldn't be able to get Max out of my mind.

"Hello there," a shrill voice said from the doorway of the shop.

I looked up with surprise. Usually I noticed someone entering before they had to approach me.

"How can I help you?" I asked with a warm smile.

The woman who stepped inside was thin to the point of appearing fragile. She appeared to be somewhere in her seventies, with short ivory curls that framed her face like flower petals.

"I just want to browse," she said and made her way into the shop area of the laundromat.

It wasn't too often that someone came in just to shop. Usually people started their laundry and then looked around. I also did laundry for customers, including sorting and folding. But this woman seemed to be intent on simply shopping.

She was studying each item in turn.

"Is there something in particular you're looking for?" I asked as I walked into the shop after her.

"I'll know it when I see it," she said with confidence.

I smiled and leaned back against the low table that served as a spot for the register and as a place to fold the laundry.

"Let me know if you need any help," I said, not wanting to disturb her as she browsed.

"Aha!" the woman said as she picked up a small green glass frog off the table. It was an item I had run across at a yard sale and thought would add a little color to our selection. "This is it," she said, grinning.

I smiled. "What's so special about the glass frog?" I asked her as she turned it over to check the price. It was only fifty cents.

"It isn't the frog that's special," the woman explained. She fished in her purse to find two quarters. "It's the memories that it brings back." She pressed the quarters into the palm of my hand. "Those are priceless."

I closed my hand around the coins and looked into her eyes. "If you don't mind me asking, what are the memories?"

"I once lived near a creek. I wasn't married yet and I had just started my first job—and I had my first lover." She blushed a little as she glanced away from me and looked down at the little green frog. "It was summer and the frogs were out. They were hopping everywhere. He would meet me on the dock and we would spend hours talking, chasing frogs, and watching the fireflies come out."

"That sounds wonderful," I said. "I can see why you would want to remember it."

"It *was* wonderful," the woman agreed. "For as long as it lasted."

"I take it you didn't stay together, then?"

"No, we didn't." She shook her head. "The thing was—he wasn't ready."

"Did he tell you that?"

"Not in so many words," the woman continued. "There's a feeling you get when you know without question what you'd do to be with someone, but deep down, you know that it's not the same for them. He was a good man, but he wasn't the marrying type. And I wasn't the type to waste my summers waiting for him to change." She winked at me. "I guess you could say it was my first love and my first heart-break, all wrapped up in this tiny little frog." She gave it a playful peck. "Not my prince, but someone I'd never want to forget."

I was fascinated by her story. I had picked up the frog to add color; she had picked up the frog because it filled her mind with memories from decades before.

By the time I came out of the enchanted state I was in, she was almost out the door.

"Wait," I called out and hurried after her.

"Is something wrong?" she asked. "Did I forget to pay?"

"No, you paid," I assured her with a smile. "I was just wondering—you said that he wasn't your prince—does that mean that you found your prince?"

"Princes aren't what they used to be." She laughed a

little. "But I did marry the love of my life, a man I never would have met if I hadn't let my heart get broken first."

"Thank you for sharing your story with me."

"Thank you for the frog," she said with a smile, and then continued down the block.

As I began to go through the motions of closing the shop up for the night, I had a strange feeling in the pit of my stomach.

Was Max my frog?

And worse—was I just someone else's summer memory?

TEN

By the time I got back to my apartment, my mind was made up. I would always have my memories of Max—and I hoped that I'd always have his friendship—but I wasn't going to waste any more summers on him.

"That's it," I said with conviction. "Time to think about the next thing on my list."

I went to my bedroom and pulled the list back out. I put a big checkmark right next to pole dancing. I thought that it had been very successful, despite the ripped leotard.

There was something very liberating about becoming more comfortable with my body. It wasn't about attracting a man, not even Max. It was about who I was and who I wanted to be. I still had some pounds to lose, but what was more important to me was gaining confidence, and I could feel mine growing stronger every day.

I had an entire list to get through, and I was ready to really set off on this journey with a new determination to change my life. I had started out my day feeling nervous and uncertain, but now I was getting to the point of wanting even more than what was already written on the list.

I added a few notes to the bottom, then hesitated as my hand hovered over Max's name. For fourteen years I'd been waiting for his romantic attention, and there was no way he didn't know it. He had to see the blush in my cheeks, the shine in my eyes, when I looked at him.

I decided it was time to cross his name off the list. As I did, I felt my heart crack—not shatter, not collapse. Just shift.

Maybe that was what growth felt like.

As I set the pencil down, my cell phone beeped. I picked it up and scanned the text I'd received from Max.

I still want to see the list. It's going to drive me crazy with curiosity.

I stared at the text for a moment. I didn't want to show him the list, that was for sure. I could erase him from my fantasies, but I could never erase him from my heart. We shared too much history, and there was too much support there. I still needed Max.

I texted him back quickly before I could dwell on my words.

Be a little crazy, see how it feels.

I smiled as I set the phone down on the bed beside me. I knew he probably wouldn't understand what I meant, but he had been driving me crazy for too many years. Letting him be the one yearning could be very therapeutic.

As I looked back down at my list, I shifted my attention to the next item. In order to accomplish it, I was going to have to recruit some assistance. I folded up the list carefully and tucked it inside a small box that had once held a bracelet. Then I placed the box inside the drawer of my bedside table.

I changed into a loose T-shirt and sweats and stepped out of my apartment.

I took a deep breath and walked four steps to the right. I paused in front of my next-door neighbor's door. It was lined with all kinds of band stickers. I didn't know who any of them were.

After a few firm knocks, the door swung open. A woman, barely edging over five feet and wearing a long black dress, opened the door. She rested her porcelain cheek against the frame and stared at me from beneath tons of eye make-up.

"What do you want?" she asked and lifted one pencil-thin, pitch-black eyebrow.

"I need your help," I said quickly.

"My help?" She eyed me and I could feel her suspicion. "Do you finally want that makeover I've been offering?"

"No—well, not right now," I added when she gave me a reproachful look. "What I need your help with is a little more technical."

"Okay, come in," she said and stepped back from the door.

I stepped through the doorway and smiled as the black-light illumination inside her apartment washed over me, reminding me again of my pole dancing class and my unexpected walk on the wild side with my little leotard malfunction.

#2 START A BLOG

ONE

I shifted from one foot to the other, doing my very best not to back out of this. I'd already asked for my neighbor's help and she'd agreed, but that didn't mean that I wasn't getting cold feet.

As a self-declared tech goddess, Kat had an apartment filled with all kinds of interesting gadgets. She had lots of action figures from science-fiction movies. She also had a ton of books. One corner of her living room was dedicated entirely to technology. She had a corner-shaped desk, with three flat-screen monitors set up.

I knew that for what I wanted to do, she was going to be the person who could help me. I wasn't used to asking for help, but Kat didn't seem to mind.

"Alright, here's some green tea," Kat said as she walked back in from the kitchen and handed me a mug.

The scent that wafted from it did not remind me of green tea. It reminded me of regret and possibly lawn clippings.

Not wanting to offend her—or appear "less than cool"—I drank it anyway.

"I can't tell you how excited I am," Kat said with a big grin. "I've been waiting and waiting for this day."

"It's not like I'm attempting something earth-shattering, is it?" I laughed a little, hoping that my less than average technical skills would be able to get the job done.

Kat plopped down in front of her computer, rubbing her hands together as if she could hardly contain her excitement. "I get to be the one who introduces you to the great beyond. Never mind that you're about ten years behind in technology. All of that can be changed in the blink of an eye."

"I hope so." I pulled over a spare chair so that I could sit beside her.

Computers were something I'd avoided in general. I didn't get the point of most social media. But now I was starting to.

"Just remember you don't have to do everything all at once. We'll get you started off slow, and as you get more comfortable with it, we can move forward. Baby steps." She smiled.

"All I want to do is start a blog." I sighed and shook my head. "I hope it's not too complicated."

"Oh, sweetie, it isn't *just* a blog." Kat turned to face me. "It's your heart—on the net!'

"Okay..." I furrowed a brow. "What do you mean?"

"I mean no one *just* has a blog. It's a place to express your feelings, your opinions, your hopes, your dreams." She smiled. "It's the last honest place on the Internet."

"I don't know if it's all of that," I said, feeling slightly over-my-head already. "I mean, I was just going to talk about my goals. I have this bucket list that I put together—of all the things I would do once I started losing weight and gaining more confidence. I thought it might be interesting for others to read about my journey."

"It's a clever concept"—Kat nodded—"but it's not enough. People read blogs written by people that they connect with. You have to be willing to *show* yourself."

"I was afraid of that." I frowned as I let her words sink in. "I think I can do it, though."

"Good. So I'll set you up with a Wordpress blog." Her fingers were already tapping away on the keyboard.

"Okay, if you're sure that's the way to go," I said, watching as a web page popped up on the screen.

"Yes, it's pretty popular right now." Kat shrugged. "Of course by next week it might be obsolete, but it's a good place to start. So what do you want your name to be?"

"I guess... Samantha?"

"Are you nuts?" Kat looked at me like she did, in fact, think I was a little crazy.

"No?" I was already feeling confused.

"You can't use your real name. The Internet is full of weirdos. You have to be careful when you're putting yourself out there. You don't want some creep showing up on your doorstep." Kat turned her attention back to the monitor.

"That wouldn't be good," I said, shaking my head. "Alright, let's see... how about Single Female on a Mission?"

"So are you—like—a die-hard bible thumper?" Kat looked at me with a look of clear disapproval. "No good."

"This is so hard." I frowned. Who knew my little idea was going to be so complicated?

"Whoa, seriously—no meltdowns. You haven't even thought of a username yet." Kat grinned. "Take a deep breath. Just think about what you want your blog to say to people."

I sat back as I thought about it. I knew that when I'd written "start a blog" on my bucket list, I had the intention of sharing my journey. But with whom? And what exactly *was* my journey? It certainly wasn't just about weight loss. I *had* lost about seventy pounds, but that wasn't the point exactly. The point was living without that weight. The point was adjusting to life in a new body. It had to be about *all* of me, not just the physical aspect of getting smaller.

"I've got it!" I said, feeling excited. "Single Wide Female!"

TWO

Kat was looking at me with an odd expression on her face. "Seriously?"

"Is there something wrong with it?" I braced myself for her response, because I was already loving the idea.

"No, not really." Kat typed in the username. "It has a ring to it. I've just never heard someone describe themselves as wide before. I mean, you *have* lost quite a bit of weight."

"It's not about my size," I said. "It's about living wide. I want my mind wide open. I want my life wide open."

"Ah, now that makes a little more sense to me." She nodded with approval. "Next you want to create a password. It should be something only you would know, but also something you won't easily forget. You don't want to have to keep resetting it. I'll let you type it in, so I won't know it either."

"Oh, I don't mind."

"Well, you should," Kat said. "This is important to you; it should be impenetrable, even by your quite helpful neighbor."

"Okay." My fingertips hovered over the keyboard for a few seconds as I considered what to use as a password. Of course it wasn't a real question. I used the same password for just about everything. I carefully typed in "Hawaii."

Because nothing says "high security" like the name of the one vacation where I almost confessed my love to my best friend and didn't.

"Great," Kat said, her voice bringing me back to the present task at hand. "Now we can choose things like colors, borders, whether you want to add pictures—most bloggers these days include photographs of themselves. It adds to the intimacy of the blog."

"I don't know about that." I couldn't help but cringe at the idea. "I don't think I have any pictures of myself that I'd like to share right now."

"No worries, you can add them at any time. Just take a nice selfie and we'll upload it later."

"Okay."

As we went through the details of setting up the blog I was actually getting excited. It was really happening—another item to check off on my list. For once, I'd have a place to spill all of my feelings and emotions—a place that wasn't in Max's ear.

Max, whom I adored, but who would never be more than a friend. I trusted him, but I needed an outlet, a place where I could speak freely without concerns about my crush or our long history.

"Okay, so you're all set." Kat nodded. "See, that wasn't too painful, was it?" She smiled.

"Not *too* painful," I said as I watched Kat write a few things down on a piece of paper that she then handed to me.

"Just follow these steps and start typing your heart out. Look"—she pointed to the monitor that still had my new blog showing on the screen—"I'm already your first follower." She grinned.

"I'm honored." I laughed.

"Just remember me when you go viral," Kat said. "That's all I ask."

I wasn't entirely sure what "viral" meant, but I hoped it didn't require antibiotics.

"Viral?" I raised an eyebrow.

Kat laughed and shook her head. "That's a lesson for another day." She walked me to the door. "Good luck, Samantha—blogging can be very therapeutic."

As I stepped out into the hallway I wondered what she was implying. Did she think I needed therapy?

"Stop obsessing, Sam," I said under my breath as I walked the few steps to the door of my apartment. I had a tendency to take things the wrong way, especially when I was feeling nervous.

I wasn't going to let my fear stop me. I thought about the pole dancing class I'd taken—the first item that I'd checked off of my bucket list. If I could do *that,* how hard could writing a blog be?

Back inside my apartment, I switched my cell phone off, determined not to have any interruptions. I changed into comfortable pants so that I wouldn't feel restrained in any way. Then I sat down with my computer in the living room.

searched through my bedside table. I ducked into my closet and began digging in my extra purses. I'd been known, on occasion, to smoke a cigarette after having a drink or two—and if I *was* smoking, I inevitably stole someone's lighter by accident.

Finally, I found one in the velvet black clutch I'd used last New Year's Eve. I smiled as I flicked the lighter on. The flame that ignited burned strong. I was sure that I was ready now.

Glancing at the clock near my bed, I was surprised that it had been almost thirty minutes since I'd set out to write the blog post.

Now my closet was trashed, with purses flung in all directions, so of course I needed to tidy it up.

I was excellent at procrastinating.

THREE

I hurried back into the living room and picked up the candle to light it, but I had to stick my hand deep into the glass jar to get to the wick. "Ouch!" The flame singed my finger. "This makes no sense," I muttered, feeling frustrated.

Finally, I managed to get the wick lit and set the candle down on the coffee table. I flopped back down on the sofa, almost knocking my computer off the cushion beside it, catching it just before it could hit the floor.

I stared at the silver surface of my laptop and shook my head. I hadn't even opened the computer and I was already exhausted.

Maybe this was a bad idea. I frowned as I moved the computer onto my lap. I thought of the list folded up safely in a box inside a drawer in my bedroom. I knew that if I started skipping out on things now, I was never going to accomplish everything.

With a renewed feeling of determination, I flipped the lid

open on the computer. It took me another twenty minutes to find and log in to the blog that Kat had set up for me.

"Okay, here I go," I said, stretching my fingers.

My hands hovered over the keyboard. I might not be up on technology, but I could type. Several years of college classes had taught me that.

I just had no idea *what* to type. I couldn't think of a single event in my life that would interest someone else.

Of course there was plenty I could write about that seemed interesting to me, but that didn't mean anyone else would understand it. I didn't do much other than my work at Fluff and Stuff and hanging out with Max—when he wasn't busy with one of his many girlfriends.

Writing a blog was supposed to be inspirational, not pathetic.

I sighed and sat back against the sofa. Maybe the problem wasn't that I couldn't think of anything to write about, but that I had *nothing interesting* to write about. I needed more experiences to share. I needed more *life* in my life.

I glanced at the time, realizing that I had to leave for work in the next ten minutes. What I'd expected would take me no more than fifteen minutes, had taken up several hours now. I just couldn't even begin to think of the first word to type.

Maybe something at work will spark my creativity.

There was actually a good chance of that. I loved my job as manager of Fluff and Stuff. The concept of the laundromat combined with the variety shop was quite creative, and there was no shortage of interesting customers coming in and out all day.

I grabbed a notebook and pen so that I could jot down any thoughts I might have while I was there, and headed out.

The laundromat was only a few blocks from my apartment, and I realized that this was probably one of the reasons that I didn't have more to blog about. I saw the same faces each day—visited the same places each day. I couldn't remember the last time I did or went somewhere brand new.

As I stepped into the shop, I waved to Helen, who was covering the early shift.

"Not much action so far," she called out as she hurried out the door.

She had to pick up her kids from school. *She* had other places to be.

I didn't really have any place that I absolutely had to be.

It wasn't until after she was long gone that I realized that she hadn't been completely honest with me. Just about all of the dryers were running with loads that would need to be folded. Normally, I'd be irritated, but today I could use the distraction.

I went into automatic mode and began emptying and folding dryer after dryer of clothes. As I was folding the last laundry order, I noticed a folded-up newspaper that someone had left behind. I picked it up to have a quick peek, looking for any events I might like to attend.

I found the Arts and Leisure section and began looking over my options. There were a few museum and art events that looked like they could be fun. I jotted down the information for a few of them.

As I was doing this, a regular customer walked through

the door. Barry was in his early twenties and liked to hang out while he did his laundry.

"Hi, Barry," I said, turning the page of the newspaper.

"Hey, Sam, what are you up to?" he asked and heaved a large laundry basket up onto one of the folding tables.

"I'm just looking for something to do this evening. I never knew there were so many activities around here."

"Activities?" he asked, while sorting through his laundry.

"Sure, there are art walks, musical acts, museum fundraisers..."

"Oh, *those* kinds of activities," he said with a nod. "There's always something going on every weekend. Of course, it's usually the older crowd," he added as he tossed some of his clothes into an empty washer.

I raised an eyebrow as I looked over at him. "Well, I *am* older," I said in what I hoped was a confident tone.

"You?" He laughed a little as he turned back to face me. "How old could you be?"

I stared at him for a moment. "In my thirties."

"Thirties?" He looked genuinely surprised. I took that as a compliment.

"Is that so surprising?" I asked with a sweet smile.

"Well, I mean, you just don't exactly act like you're in your thirties," he said.

He hadn't thought I was younger because of my looks, he thought I was younger because of my behavior. "Gee, thanks." I didn't bother to hide my annoyance.

"Oh, please, I didn't mean to offend you." He rolled his eyes and laughed again. "There's nothing wrong with being in your thirties. In fact, my aunt is thirty-five and she still goes out every weekend."

I looked at him, my eyes wide. "As opposed to sitting inside and knitting?" I asked in my most sarcastic tone. "Most thirty-somethings are out and about, you know."

"I guess." He shrugged. "My point is that she goes to this wine thing every weekend near Weston Avenue. There's a gallery there that features local artists. Afterwards, they have a wine tasting. I'm pretty sure my aunt just goes for the wine." He laughed.

"Well, wine is a good enough excuse." I smiled, feeling less irritated and more curious about this event that Barry was talking about.

Going out on the town would be good for me.

As the last wave of customers came in to pick up their laundry, I didn't even notice that Barry had slipped out.

Soon Fluff and Stuff was empty again.

I hadn't come up with any ideas for the blog, but I was hoping that my evening would bring something of interest.

I tidied up the small shop and made sure that everything was in its place. I had picked out many of the unique second-hand items myself; as I glanced at them, I imagined that each one had its own story to tell—no doubt much more interesting than any stories I could come up with in my own life—a sad fact that I was determined to change as soon as possible.

FOUR

I walked back to my apartment deep in thought. I wanted to make sure that I didn't miss a single opportunity to be interesting. I was reinventing myself, after all, and I wanted the new me to be sophisticated and cultured, not someone who would be thought of as younger.

Thinking of my earlier conversation with Barry made me cringe, and I vowed to get started that very night by checking out the gallery event we'd talked about.

When I walked into my bedroom, I saw it differently.

I saw the teddy bear I still had from my childhood, still sitting on the corner shelf. I saw the bedspread covered with flowers, with tiny little fairies peeking out from behind the petals. On the wall hung an old school bulletin board pinned with memories—mostly pictures of Max and me.

I sighed, realizing that I had the bedroom of a teenage girl.

A teenage girl who was still waiting for her life to start.

There was nothing alluring or sensual about the room I

slept in. There was nothing sophisticated or interesting, only the remnants of my youth that had passed me by.

I think it was time that I faced this fact.

I made my way over to my closet and grabbed an empty box from beneath the hanging clothes. I turned back to my room and began a cleansing.

In the box went the blanket. In the box went the teddy bear and down came the bulletin board. I tossed the bulletin board down onto the smooth surface of the bright blue sheets that the blanket had been covering. Who had blue sheets anyway?

I made a mental note to buy new ones the next day.

As I looked down at the pictures on the bulletin board, I couldn't bring myself to throw them away.

One by one, I took the pictures off the bulletin board.

There was a picture of Max and me together at Fluff and Stuff when we had just started working there. Another was of Max in his swimsuit as we prepared to run into the waves on our tropical vacation. In another picture, Max was gazing sadly down at something in his hands. It was taken a few days after his father's funeral, and though it couldn't be seen in the photograph, I knew that he was holding his father's watch.

These pictures were more than just my youth. They were the real memories that I cherished—things that were important to me. I piled the pictures up and tucked them into the drawer beside the little box that held my bucket list. Then I swept all of the fruity scented candles off my bureau and into the big box on the floor.

I was determined more than ever to become somebody that someone would want to read about.

I returned the box to the bottom of my closet. I grabbed a little black dress to wear.

Once I had it on and smoothed down I braved looking in the mirror. One big difference between a thin woman and a bigger woman trying on clothes was the anticipation. A thin woman might anticipate looking fabulous, while I anticipated looking like a penguin.

However, the mirror revealed that my weight loss did show. The dress actually complimented the curves of my figure. Tonight was going to be an amazing night. I wasn't going to let anything stop me from being the woman I should have been long ago.

I pinned my hair back into a neat bun at the curve of my head and smiled at my reflection.

I called a taxi, then gathered my purse, my keys, and my phone. I checked to make sure that my phone was fully charged, as I knew that I would need pictures to document my experiences.

The evening was balmy, and I was glad, as the dress I was wearing was on the lighter, skimpier side.

I waited only a few minutes for the taxi to arrive. When I slid across the vinyl seat, the cab driver looked through the rear view mirror at me.

"Where to?" he asked.

"Wherever I can find some real culture," I said, smiling.

He gazed at me from beneath heavy eyebrows with his lips drawn in a thin straight line. He didn't look amused or open to helping me out.

"Weston Avenue." I sat back in my seat.

FIVE

As the cab driver drove away from my neighborhood, I studied the people walking on the sidewalks. There was such a variety, from people dressed in expensive clothing to people dressed in ratty old jeans. There was no dress code for the street; everyone got to wear what they pleased. Each person had their own destination that night, and I had to wonder how many were heading to the gallery.

"You can drop me off here." I pointed to an art walk that had been set up along the sidewalk a few blocks from the gallery.

"Twenty," he said as he applied the brakes.

"Twenty?" I knew that he was overcharging me, but I was determined not to care. I handed him the twenty-dollar bill and climbed out of the taxi.

There was a small crowd gathered around the entrance of the art walk. I could hear snippets of conversation combined with polite laughter. It was definitely not a party scene. I hoped that I could blend in well. I'd never been the most skilled when it came to social situations. I could do "cheerful and bubbly" but when it came down to real intellectual conversation, I was always a little too nervous.

I walked up to a man who was standing at the entrance of the art walk.

"Is there a cost?"

He looked back at me with his long pointed nose slightly scrunched up.

"Isn't there always?" he said.

I stared at him blankly.

He laughed and the sound was so abrasive that it startled me. "Donations are accepted," he said. "But not required."

I smiled, feeling slightly nervous as I reached into my purse. I never knew how much a donation should be. If I gave too much would I look like a show-off? If I gave too little would I be insulting the artist?

Considering I hadn't even seen the paintings yet, I handed the man a ten.

"The artist thanks you," he said, smiling as he tucked the ten-dollar bill into a small donation box.

I felt a little more confident as I began to walk along, looking at the paintings. Each one depicted a group of people. One even featured a group of people at what appeared to be an art walk. Some were gathered at a mall. Some were in various states of repose around a lake. Others were waiting in line at a shop or sitting in a bus.

The artwork was good enough, but it was nothing spectacular. They just seemed like normal-life scenes to me. I frowned as I studied one of the last paintings. It was a group of children at a playground. They were all smiling and laughing with one another. It was a nice painting.

"Profound, isn't it?" a woman said as she walked up beside me.

She was dressed in a sleek silver dress that seemed to be tailored to enhance the shape of her body. Her hair was flawless. Her make-up was just enough.

I felt awkward as I looked over at her. I didn't really see anything profound about the painting.

"To think that she did this over the span of a year, and this is the only one."

I really had no idea what the woman was talking about. I didn't want to sound uninformed, but I also didn't want to miss out on the point of the collection.

"Only one?" I asked and raised an eyebrow.

The woman regarded me for a moment, then a look of realization crossed her delicate features. "Oh, you don't get it," she said with a soft laugh. I must have blushed, because she rested a hand lightly on my shoulder. "Don't worry, neither did I at first. This particular artist set out to do voyeur scenes of the expressions of people as they interacted with each other. She visited several different locations over a year in an attempt to capture those intimate moments between people. But she couldn't seem to find anyone who was actually looking at one another"—she gestured to the paintings I had already walked past. "If you look at them again, you'll see that no one is facing another person. No one seems to be talking or interacting with anyone else."

"Really?" I said, surprised. "I didn't even notice that."

"No one does," the woman said. "The artist herself explained it to me, that's why I know."

"But this last one?" I pointed to the painting in front of us.

"The only one." The woman nodded. "Children look at each other in the face. They laugh with each other. They look into each other's eyes. That was what the artist was trying to point out—that at some point for some reason we stop seeing one another."

I smiled. "That really is profound," I said quietly.

"Yes, it is." The woman smiled back at me.

"Do you think it's real or do you think the artist just staged it?" It was hard for me to believe that people in so many different places didn't bother to even look at one another.

"I honestly don't know. But I also don't think it really matters. I mean, it speaks to you, doesn't it?" she asked. "These days, what do you do if you want to meet someone new? Is there somewhere you can go where it's acceptable to just walk up and introduce yourself and ask to be friends?" She laughed a little. "We leave that honesty behind on the playground."

"I guess you're right," I said, feeling rather reflective about the whole conversation.

SIX

I couldn't imagine just meeting someone in the grocery store or while out for a walk.

As I turned back to face the woman, inspired to introduce myself, I found that she'd already walked off.

I looked back at the painting of the children. It struck me that maybe being mature wasn't the best thing in the world. Was it age that isolated us from one another, or insecurity?

With these thoughts on my mind I walked toward the gallery. I was looking forward to getting a selfie outside the building so that I could prove that I was there.

I paused outside and fidgeted with my phone.

I hadn't mastered the art of taking a good selfie. Usually I ended up with one eye half shut or a clear view of the inside of my nostril. Determined to make it great for my blog, I practiced a few different expressions. When I heard a smothered laugh, I looked to my right to find that a small line had formed behind me. I was blocking the entrance of the gallery and everyone waiting was being treated to my selfie practice.

"Sorry." Embarrassed, I started to move out of the way.

Right at that moment I hit the button on my phone.

Once everyone had walked past me with strange and amused looks, I checked the picture. I'd managed to capture one half-shut eye, one enthusiastic nostril, and teeth that could have starred in a toothpaste cautionary tale.

I sighed and went to delete the picture; however, as I was hitting the button to delete it, someone jostled past me to get into the gallery and my hand bounced across the screen.

I saw the confirmation: *Sent.*

My eyes widened as I wondered who in the world I had sent such a horrible picture to. I checked my texts to discover that in the midst of everything, Max had sent me a text.

What are you up to, beautiful?

In response I had inadvertently sent him back the most hideous picture I'd ever taken of myself.

"Oh no." I groaned and started to send a text explaining the situation.

Before I could get it typed Max had sent me another text.

Sexy.

I glared at the phone and turned it off. I knew he was teasing me.

I decided to forget about the selfie and continue with my evening.

As I stepped into the gallery, I willed myself to act cultured.

The gallery wasn't very crowded. I was a little surprised to see that it featured photographs rather than paintings. The images were quite breathtaking, if not a little mind-boggling. It took me several minutes to figure out that what I was looking at in one photograph was a single flower petal. The artist seemed whimsical and playful.

There was one thing that Barry had been right about. The crowd *was* on the older side. Most looked to be in their early fifties and older.

I didn't mind, though, as I was so enraptured by the photographs, I didn't have time to attempt to socialize.

I paused in front of one particular image which was the swirl of a thumbprint. I stared at it for some time. I was certain that there was some kind of wise and witty blog post that I could come up with, inspired by that photograph.

"The circles we follow," I mumbled to myself and then shook my head. "Our paths are designed before we're born, like thumbprints," I whispered to myself. I scrunched up my nose and shook my head. "Too New Age."

I sighed as I continued to study the picture. I wished that it could just talk to me—give me something to write about.

"It's amazing, isn't it?" a smooth voice asked from beside me.

I was startled, as I hadn't even noticed that someone had come to stand next to me.

He was a tall man, slender and dressed impeccably. His hair was a mixture of blond and silver. He looked to be in his late forties, perhaps a little older. His expression was serene as he continued to study the photograph.

"It's endless, eternal, and yet minuscule." He smiled, looking very pleased with himself.

In three words he had summed up everything I had been feeling about the photograph. I was enchanted as I met his eyes.

"I was just thinking that," I said with a nervous smile.

"Oh?" he asked. "Well, I guess great minds think alike." He smiled.

"Maybe they do," I said. "I'm Samantha."

"Ronald," he replied and tipped his head slightly in my direction. "It's a pleasure to meet you, Samantha. There are many great works to see here. Are you a fan of the artist?"

"Actually, this is my first time seeing the work." I smiled, feeling slightly nervous and awkward. "I really just came for the wine." I laughed much too loudly.

My joke obviously fell on deaf ears; I noticed his eyes narrow.

"I see," he said under his breath as he started to turn away.

"I'm sorry. What I meant was that I didn't even know that these shows existed until tonight," I called out to him.

"Well, now you do," he said with a soft smile before walking toward the next photograph.

I didn't want to follow him, potentially giving off the stalker vibe. He was so distinguished. I was certain that he would have a million things to put in a blog.

I looked back at the photograph. The thumb looked like it was mocking me.

"I'll tell you where you can stick that thumb," I said under my breath as I moved on to the next display.

SEVEN

As I studied each photograph, I waited for an epic thought to enter my mind. Something that would make a reader stop and say, *Wow, this girl really has it all figured out.* But my mind filled with thoughts of hot dogs, cheeseburgers, and a chef's salad large enough to emotionally support me.

I was starving. My stomach had begun to growl. I hoped that I was the only one who could hear it.

As if on cue, they began handing out the wine. One thing I'd learned from dieting was that it was *not* a good idea to drink wine on an empty stomach. I'd had the worst hangover of my life one time after skipping all the high-calorie treats at a wedding so that I could focus on the wine.

I turned quickly and tried to duck out the front door of the gallery. I was sure there had to be a vendor of some kind out on the street. Just a quick hot dog or pretzel would help me soak up the wine I was looking forward to drinking.

When I reached the door, I found a couple standing in

front of it. They were talking softly to one another. They stared deeply into each other's eyes.

I was stunned by the way they never looked away, not even to laugh or offer a smile. It was as if they were only aware of each other.

I didn't want to interrupt that. I wanted to *be* that. I wanted someone to find *me* that fascinating.

When a waiter walked by to offer me a glass of wine, I snatched it off the tray, downing it in three decisive swallows, like I was preparing for competitive regret.

"Oops." I frowned as I felt the sudden heat hit my cheeks.

"Didn't you get a glass of wine?" another waiter asked with concern. He handed me another glass before I could answer.

I noticed that I had drawn a few stares from other patrons because of my wine guzzling.

Everyone else was taking their time, going through the process of tasting their wine, rather than chugging it like a frat boy.

I cleared my throat and did my best to follow the same steps that I saw other people taking.

I attempted to swirl the wine in my glass; however, the wine refused to stay *in* the glass. Instead, it splashed over the brim and all over my hand. I cringed as the cool liquid covered my palm. I looked around for a napkin, but before I could find one, a man stepped up beside me. It was the same suave gentleman that had drawn my attention earlier.

"Enjoying your wine?" he asked.

"Well, I was," I said with a slight laugh.

Before I realized what he was doing he took the glass from my hand. He sniffed the wine carefully.

"Is it off?" he asked with some concern. His steel-blue eyes looked up from the wine and back at me intently.

"No, it's not that. It's just I—" I started to explain.

"No matter." He took my hand in his own. "I'll get you another—um," he drew his hand out of mine and shook it a little. "You seem to, uh—"

"It's wine," I said quickly—too quickly.

He smiled strangely and handed me back my glass.

"Enjoy it," he said and turned to walk away.

I wanted to call out to him, to force him to understand that it was the wine on my palm, not sweat, or some other random sticky substance. But there was no point. I had tried all day long to be more cultured, to be interesting and even a little wise.

In the end, all I had was a bunch of silly selfies and wine on my hand.

I downed the remainder of my wine and then dropped the glass on one of the passing trays.

The couple by the door no longer fascinated me. In fact, they were annoying.

"Don't you ever blink?" I asked as I shouldered past them and out through the door.

Neither seemed to even notice my drunken, disparaging comment.

Outside, the air had grown cool. I knew that I could spend a little more time wandering the sidewalks, looking for inspiration, but I felt completely dull. My evening out had only proven that I didn't fit into cultured society, and as a result, I wasn't going to have anything interesting to share on my blog.

I started walking back towards my apartment, thinking that a brisk walk might do me some good.

I'd only walked a few blocks when my stomach began to churn. I rubbed my hand over it and moaned quietly. The wine was beginning to fight back. I glanced around to see if there were any shops or restaurants available. Everything was either closed or didn't offer food.

I wasn't sure if I was going to make it. I knew I wouldn't make it all the way home.

I leaned back against the wall of a building and closed my eyes. The world began to spin around me. I knew the moment I opened my eyes I was going to have to vomit.

"Sammy, what are you doing out here?" Max asked from a few feet in front of me.

My eyes opened by instinct, and my stomach clenched tightly in preparation for revolt.

I shoved Max hard out of my way just in time.

EIGHT

All of the wine was now out of me and onto the pavement.

"Sorry." I was mortified.

Max handed me a tissue to wipe my mouth. "Wine on an empty stomach?" he asked and raised an eyebrow.

I nodded a little as I wiped at my mouth.

"When are you going to learn, Sammy?" he asked with a slight laugh. "Are you okay?"

"I think so." I sighed. "What are you doing here?" I asked when my head finally stopped swirling.

"You didn't text me back. I tried calling you and your phone was off. I figured you were mad or abducted, so I went to look for you at the gallery. Someone there told me you walked off this way."

"How did they know who you were looking for?" I asked. Then my eyes widened.

"Oh no, you didn't, did you?" I stared at him with horror.

"Well, it was the most recent picture I had of you—and good job getting just the hint of the event sign in there along with your eye and nostril, which gave me a clue at least." He laughed. "I'm glad to see that you weren't abducted. So does that mean that you're mad?" He pouted a little.

"No," I sighed and leaned back against the wall. "I'm not mad. I'm just a complete failure."

Which felt dramatic, but also extremely accurate in the moment.

"Failure? What are you talking about?"

"I came out here tonight to get a little culture, but I only succeeded in making a fool of myself—as usual." I frowned.

"Oh, listen to you." He rolled his eyes and grabbed my hand. "What you need is food. Let's go. There's a little hole-in-the-wall restaurant a few blocks up."

"I don't know if I should eat," I said as I rubbed my stomach.

"That means that you absolutely do need to eat."

As we walked, I felt so much comfort with Max beside me. Even though our relationship was such a conflict in my mind, he still soothed me in ways that no one else could. But I couldn't put that in my blog. My blog needed to be Max-free.

"I guess I could eat a little," I said and then sighed.

"What were you even doing out here?" he asked as we walked toward the restaurant. "This isn't where you usually hang out. Were you really trying to fit in?"

"I didn't think it would be that much of a stretch." I laughed lightly. "I just wanted to learn to be interesting."

"Learn to be interesting?" He laughed at that as he held the door of the restaurant open for me.

"Is that funny?" I asked, as we settled in a small booth to wait for the waitress.

"It's not that it's funny so much as that it's absurd."

"It's not absurd," I said. "Fries and a coke," I ordered when the waitress walked up.

"Bring her a cheeseburger too," Max said. "I'll take one as well and a beer. Whatever dark you have."

"Why do you always do that?" I asked, not bothering to hide my frustration.

"Do what?"

"Order things for me. If I wanted a cheeseburger, I would have ordered a cheeseburger.," I kept my voice low, but I was annoyed.

He sat back in his seat and studied me across the table. "No, you wouldn't."

"I wouldn't what?"

"You wouldn't order a cheeseburger if you wanted one," he said, looking way too confident.

"Of course I would," I said.

"No, you wouldn't. I see you do it all the time. You'll tell me you're so hungry, and when we go to the restaurant you order a tiny little meal. French fries aren't even a meal," he pointed out with a frown.

"Maybe not, but that's what I wanted."

"Oh?" He leaned forward and rested his elbows on the table. He looked me directly in the eye. "So you had no desire for a hot, meaty cheeseburger?" he asked in a slow sultry tone.

"Oh my God, I hate you." I frowned and crossed my arms.

"That's not nice," he said, teasing me. "Just tell me I'm right, and we can enjoy our meal."

I frowned. I didn't want to tell him that he was right, but the truth was, he was. I tended to order small when I was feeling insecure. It was odd, but I sometimes felt as if people were staring at me, judging me for what I ate. So I would order something I didn't necessarily want.

"Fine," I finally admitted. "I did want a cheeseburger."

"See?" He shrugged. "So what's the problem?"

"The problem is that I can order for myself," I reminded him, though our argument felt like it was going in circles.

"No," he said. "The problem is that you can't order for yourself. Just like you spent an evening trying to be something you're not. Why? That's what you should figure out." He sat back as our meals were placed in front of us.

The cheeseburger looked delicious, but Max's words stuck in my mind. He was pointing out a pattern that I'd never really noticed before. Darn, but he could be insightful.

"Fine, maybe it's true," I said, my voice low. "You should know, after all."

"What's that supposed to mean?" he asked, looking up at me.

"Like the women you date," I said and took a casual sip of my Coke.

"What about them?"

I could sense that he was getting defensive real fast.

"You're always picking the most dull women I've ever met," I pointed out and set my glass down. "There are intelligent skinny women out there, you know."

"Wow." He shook his head and pushed his plate slightly away from him. "You're way off base."

"Am I?" I asked. "What about Gina?"

"Gina was a mistake," he frowned.

"Like you couldn't tell she would be—before you went on a date with her?" I enjoyed that it was his turn to squirm a bit now.

"Look, you don't know what you're talking about," he said. "I like to give women a chance—to see if we click."

"And if you don't, you never call them—you never follow up. Do you know what that does to a woman?"

He frowned and grabbed his cheeseburger off his plate. He took a big bite out of it and chewed it slowly.

I knew that he was just trying to delay the conversation. So I took a bite of my cheeseburger as well.

"You just don't understand." He shook his head and took a swallow of his beer.

"What don't I understand?" I asked and smiled, genuinely curious now.

NINE

Max met my eyes and set his beer back down on the table, hesitating just long enough to make me slightly nervous as to what his next words were going to be.

"They can't all be you, Sammy," he said, his voice serious.

For half a second, I let myself believe he meant it the way I wanted him to.

But in the next moment, he grinned and winked at me. All hopes that I had of his finally professing his love for me were dashed.

"Thanks, I guess," I said and drained the last of my Coke.

Even though we had shared a meal together, and he had done his best to find me when he thought I was upset or in danger, I still felt like a bit of a joke to him. I couldn't recall when, exactly, things had shifted so much between us.

"I'll walk you home," he said as we boxed up our leftovers.

"Sounds good."

We settled up with the waitress and I left a good tip. It

was better than the money I had wasted on the art walk. I thought of the man at the wine tasting and the way he had looked at me with such interest and then such judgment. I decided it had to be exhausting to be so perfect all the time.

Max looped his arm through mine and we began walking down the sidewalk to my apartment.

"How's your stomach?"

"Better now." I sighed.

"Good—so maybe now you can stick to being you, instead of trying to be someone else?"

"Who am I?" I stopped.

Since his arm was linked with mine, he stopped too.

"You tell me," he said and waited.

"I have no idea." I shook my head. "How can I be thirty-two years old and have no idea who I am?"

"I guess you've spent far too long trying to figure out who people want you to be." Max shrugged. "It's easy to get caught up in that game."

"Seems that way," I said. "Do you ever feel like you're falling behind everyone else, Max?"

"What do you mean?" he asked as we began walking again.

"I mean, everyone around us is getting married, having kids, or dogs, or something amazing like that. We're still acting like we're in our twenties," I pointed out.

"Hey, speak for yourself—I do have a fish," Max laughed.

"Have you fed it lately?" I glanced over at him.

"Uh, well..." Max frowned. "I better check on that fish."

"That's my point," I said. "Did we miss out on something? Why aren't we gravitating toward more commitment in our lives?"

"I don't know." Max shrugged. "I guess I'm just not ready to settle down yet."

"What is that?" I asked as we reached my apartment building. "What is settling down?"

"Huh—a house, a wife, a parrot." Max shrugged again.

I had to laugh at his words. But I could tell the conversation was making him uncomfortable. As much as he wanted to make it seem as if I was the one doing all the pretending, I knew that Max was hiding a lot as well.

"I guess this is good night," I said as we reached my door.

"Unless you want me to come in?" He looked over at me as I rummaged in my purse for my keys. "We could have a glass of wine."

"No," I groaned. "No more wine, maybe not ever." I unlocked the door.

"So, that's a no to coming inside too?" he said.

I glanced over at him, a little surprised. He wasn't usually so keen to hang out this late at night.

"Don't you have someone better you could spend the evening with?" I asked as I met his eyes.

"Better?" He shook his head slightly. "No. Someone different, sure. But no one better." He smiled. "You know that."

"Sure, Max. Go home," I said and shook my head.

I opened the door to my apartment and stepped inside. I started to turn back to invite him in, but when I did, he was already gone. I frowned and closed the door. It was for the best, I knew.

Being alone with Max when I was a little tipsy was probably not a good idea, considering the fantasies I frequently had about him. A little buzz could blur the lines of reality and fantasy.

However, maybe the wine I'd had had relaxed me enough to finally write my blog post.

I sat down at my computer. This time, I ignored the candles, the music, and the lighting. I just opened the darn computer, positioning my fingers over the keys.

I took a deep breath as I stared at the blinking cursor on the screen.

This time, I didn't try to think of what people would want to read. Instead, I thought about how I'd just spent my evening, trying to make myself interesting. I had to wonder how many other women felt that way—like they had some image that they were trying to live up to—that they had to work so hard to be anything other than who they truly were.

I began typing and as the words flowed out of me, I felt transformed.

I was being honest. I was making spelling errors. I was sure that my grammar would enrage someone. But it was me—all me—one hundred percent me. Not what I thought people wanted to hear, not what my mother wanted me to be, not even what Max wanted me to be. It was all of my insecurities and all of my dreams.

TEN

In my blog post, I talked about the fact that people didn't even see each other any more because we were all too busy focusing on our own flaws. The paintings had oddly taught me that.

By the time I was finished writing, I felt as if a huge burden had been lifted from my shoulders. I had released pure emotion, untainted by the perceptions or expectations of others, and it felt great.

As I read it over, I was surprised that the words had come so easily from me. I'd written about the details of my bucket list—why I'd started it—and I invited others to join me on the journey, creating their own bucket lists to conquer.

I still felt pretty uncertain about it. Sure, the words meant a lot to me, but would anyone else even care? I hoped that maybe someone would stumble across the blog and find something of meaning in it.

I hovered the mouse over the post button. I knew once I

submitted it, that would be it. My words would be floating around in cyberspace.

I hit the button and sat back.

No fireworks. No applause.

Just me... and the terrifying knowledge that the Internet now knew I existed.

I closed the computer and carried it over to the table to put away for the night.

I thought about what tomorrow might bring as I headed for my bedroom.

Would I be able to keep up with my blog? Would I be able to live without worrying about the expectations of others? For most people, I knew that wouldn't be too difficult. With Max, it was going to be rough.

As I sprawled out on my bed and stared up at the ceiling, I thought about the choices I'd been making lately. I remembered cleansing my room of all things immature. I did that because I wanted to look like someone else.

I got up out of bed and headed to the closet. I snatched my teddy bear out of the box. I set it back on the shelf where it belonged. It had gotten me through many sleepless nights, and It, too, was part of who I was.

And I was finally starting to understand that maybe I didn't need to erase pieces of myself to become interesting.

As I drifted off to sleep I felt a sense of pride at being able to check one more item off on my bucket list. Not only that, but I actually felt as if I might have stumbled upon a new talent—writing. Just when I thought there was nothing about myself that could surprise me, I discovered that I liked to write. I looked forward to discovering what else I might learn about myself during this journey.

I woke up with a headache that pulsed behind my eyes like a tiny drummer with anger issues. I groaned and tried to lift my head. It protested. Loudly.

Normally I would have stayed in bed and felt sorry for myself. But I'd posted the blog the night before. And that meant someone might have responded. Or judged me. Or both.

I forced myself up, hunted down aspirin, swallowed it with water from the sink, and splashed my face like that might magically improve my life. Then I grabbed a bottle of water and made my way to the computer, equal parts hopeful and terrified.

My computer seemed to be taunting me. I sat down and cracked open the bottle of water. I took a sip and then opened the lid. I logged in and navigated to the blog site. I was surprised to find that I already had one comment. I expected it to be from Kat and prepared myself for some fierce criticism.

I clicked on the message and began to read it.

What amazing insight you offer. You are a very wise person. If I could see the world through your eyes, I'm sure that it would seem like a more beautiful place. Thanks for sharing your words. I look forward to reading many more.

I sat back and smiled. It was a lovely comment. I had no

idea who had written it. The screen name was Blue. Nothing more, nothing less. Just Blue. I thought that was interesting.

It was a little odd to think that some stranger out there in Internet land had found a connection with me without having any idea of who I was. It was also thrilling. But more than that, I felt as if I had actually inspired someone. That was what I really wanted my blog to do.

I was still in my creative glow, when my phone began to ring. I picked it up, expecting it to be Max, or even Kat, not realizing my mistake until I heard my mother's nasal voice.

"Samantha Anne," she said with clear annoyance. "I have been calling you for over a week."

"What? I didn't get any messages."

This was not true. I had been avoiding her calls. Once a month my mother liked to take me out to dinner. Once a month she pointed out how she was still waiting for a son-in-law and grandkids.

"Sure, Samantha." she sighed. "Listen, I can't make our dinner this month. I've gotten a little too busy. I've been seeing this amazing man and—"

"What?" I asked, surprised.

My parents had split up just after I turned eighteen. My father had moved on with another wife a few years later, but my mother had never even dated.

"I know. It's a surprise, isn't it?" She laughed. "But he's just so charming."

"I'm glad, Mom," I said quietly. I was a little envious.

"Listen, Samantha, your time is going to come," she assured me. "You're like a fine wine—you getter better with age."

I cringed at the mention of wine and age. "Mom, I really don't want to have this conversation right now."

"Listen, why don't you just try getting out there and meeting some new people?"

"I tried that, Mom," I said, feeling annoyed.

"Well, when all else fails, remember, the way to a man's heart is through his stomach," she said, and I knew she was not-so-discreetly making a dig at my lack of cooking abilities. "I have to go, hon, love you."

"Love you too, Mom," I said before hanging up the phone.

I smiled because I knew what was next on my bucket list.

#3 LEARN TO COOK

ONE

Bathed in the glow of my computer screen, I felt connected to the entire world.

Okay, maybe just to one reader. Possibly one bored insomniac. But still—it felt like the whole world.

I hit submit on my latest blog entry and immediately wondered if I had just changed my life... or simply updated it.

I didn't know how many people would find the fact that I had finally decided to take my mother's advice interesting, but I hoped that there might be a few.

I walked into the kitchen.

My kitchen.

It was spotless. Not because I was organized. Not because I was domestic. But because I didn't actually cook. The microwave and toaster handled the few culinary risks I was willing to take. The oven? Untouched. Untested. Possibly confused about its purpose.

I did eat healthy these days. Lots of fresh food. I just liked it chopped, seasoned, and handed to me by someone wearing an apron. Or delivered to my door in environmentally questionable packaging.

When it came to actually turning on my stove or oven, I preferred to pick up my purse and walk out the door. My oven and I had a respectful, long-term non-relationship.

Maybe my aversion to cooking came from my mother's firm belief that a man only came running when delicious smells were drifting from the kitchen. Preferably smells created by a thin, cheerful woman in an apron.

Our house had always been filled with food, and my father had been a happy man. But they didn't exactly get along, despite all my mother's cooking. I always felt like she was telling me that the only way a man would love me was if I could cook him a meal.

I wanted a man who would love me no matter what. Or better yet, a man who would cook for me! Still single at thirty-two, that particular strategy had yet to produce results. Shocking, I know.

Fortunately, Chef Vincenzo offered a cooking class for those of us who considered boiling water an accomplishment.

Even more fortunate, I stumbled across his website while researching for my blog.

And most miraculous of all—he had an opening.

It almost felt like the universe was nudging me toward Italian cuisine and my third bucket list item.

When I heard a knock on the door, I was surprised and slightly suspicious. I didn't have many visitors, other than Max, who always let himself in with his key.

"Who is it?" I called out and slowly approached the door. I had a baseball bat stowed just for these occasions. I had never used it. I wasn't entirely sure I could swing it. But it made me feel like a responsible adult.

"It's me, Max," he called back from the other side.

My heart skipped a beat as I heard those words. Yes, I had taken "be with Max" off my bucket list, but my heart didn't seem to understand that.

I opened the door to let him in."Did you lose your key?"

"No, I didn't," he said with a shrug. "But I figured that it might be better if I knocked first."

"You don't have to knock." I smiled. "What's the worst thing that could happen—you see me naked?"

He raised an eyebrow. "Is that a possibility?"

"Highly unlikely," I said. "I don't even see me naked unless absolutely necessary. Anyway, you caught me at a bad time. I'm just heading out."

"Another adventure?" he asked as he watched me gather my things.

"Maybe..."

Max had been trying to figure out just what I was up to for quite some time. But I was determined to have at least one secret from the man who knew me better than anyone else in the world.

"Where are you off to?"

"I'm going to take a cooking class," I said as I finished loading up my purse.

"Why?"

"Because I want to learn to cook more than just waffles and macaroni and cheese," I said as I walked past him into the living room.

"Well, that sounds good." He grinned and rubbed his stomach. "I'll be happy to be your guinea pig."

"Great." I smiled. "I will keep that in mind when I burn my first official meal."

"Okay, maybe you could practice a little first." He laughed.

"Not so brave now, are you?" I winked at him. "I have to get going soon, but first you have to tell me how your date with Angela went," I said as I started toward the door.

TWO

Max flopped down on my sofa as if he had no intention of leaving. "Angela," he said and shook his head with dismay.

"That bad?" I turned to look at him. I did my best to hide my amusement, but he was being overly dramatic on purpose to keep my attention.

"It was not bad exactly, just horrendous." He sighed.

"Horrendous?" I said, thinking that Max could really be very dramatic. "I hardly think that's possible on one date."

"Look, I took your advice. I took her out to a nice meal and then we spent time walking together by the water—so that we could talk." He groaned.

"You mean you attempted to create *real* intimacy?" I teased.

Max was more of a finish-line kind of guy when it came to dating. Everything was about how fast he could get a woman back to his place. I had mentioned once or twice that it might be part of the reason he never seemed to have a second date.

"I tried," he said as he looked up at me with the gorgeous eyes that always managed to catch me by surprise. "I even thought of a clever way to learn how her mind works. I asked her to tell me three reasons why she woke up in the morning."

"Okay, Dr. Phil." I laughed a little and shook my head.

"What?" he asked. "I thought it was clever. I wanted to know what was important to her."

"Okay, fair enough," I agreed, adjusting my purse on my shoulder. "So, what did she say?"

"It was horrendous," he reminded me. "I tried to be open-minded—really I did. But she couldn't even think of one reason why she'd be excited to wake up in the morning—couldn't even bother to make up a reason." He shook his head.

"So?" I said. "Maybe you put her on the spot and she was too nervous to come up with anything."

"The only thing that she said was that she got out of bed because the alarm rings. And she was totally serious when she said it. Does that sound like a happy life to you?" He frowned. "I mean if the only reason you wake up in the morning is because of an annoying little beeping sound, doesn't that mean you have absolutely nothing to look forward to?"

"I don't think it matters what I think," I said. "But she might have been shy. Or maybe she's just at a low point in her life. Women aren't born perky, you know." I shrugged.

"Oh, she was plenty perky." He laughed.

"Oh, Max." I rolled my eyes. "That's not what I mean. What matters is who she is, not how she answers some silly question that she probably didn't even fully understand. Did you have a good time with her?"

"I guess," he said, sounding less than thrilled. "Dinner was fine. She actually ordered a real meal and she even offered to go Dutch."

"Max, you didn't, did you?" I asked, fearing the worst.

"No, of course not." He pursed his lips and then grinned at me. "You know I'm always a gentleman."

I wanted to remind him of his perky comment, but I decided to bite my tongue instead.

"You know, Max, you have a tendency to find something wrong with every woman that you date." I was trying my hardest not to sound too judgmental. "Maybe you could lower your standards a little."

"You know, Sammy, you tend not to date at all." He grinned. "Maybe you could accept a date or two."

"Ha ha." I restrained myself from kicking him.

He was right, though. I hadn't been on a real date in some time. "When the right man comes along, I'll know it."

"Don't ask him why he gets up in the morning." He laughed.

"Why do you get up in the morning, Max?" I asked as I grabbed my light jacket.

He stared at me for a long moment, then smiled. "To live my life—one adventure after another," he said, sounding confident.

"Okay, good answer, but you've had plenty of time to think about it." I shook my head. "I think you should call her back. Ask her out again."

"Nope." He shook his head. "That ship has sailed, Sammy."

I rolled my eyes. "I'm out of here."

"Alright, fine." He groaned and stood up from the sofa.

As he sauntered past me, I felt the warmth of his body close to mine. I felt the urge to wrap my arms around him, to boldly pull him into the kiss that I had been longing for—for so many years. For just a split second, I thought I actually would.

Then he winked at me, in that dismissive way that made me feel as if I was twelve.

"Have fun at your cooking class, Sam," he said when we were out on the street, lightly tugging on my hair. "Just remember that I don't like mushrooms."

"I'll remember," I said under my breath as he walked away.

I watched as he walked down the sidewalk. I wanted to convince myself that I didn't feel anything when I looked at Max. But the blare of a horn as I nearly stepped directly into traffic told me differently.

"Sorry," I called out as the driver flipped me off.

"Sam, don't play in traffic!" Max yelled over his shoulder. I glared at him.

We waved goodbye and I hailed a taxi.

On the ride to the class, I thought about the fact that I hadn't dated much.

To be honest, more often than not, if I was asked, I turned them down. Max was right. I had settled into a slump. I was hoping that the cooking class would help me get out of it.

I looked out the window at the people that we were

speeding by. Lately, it seemed as if everyone I saw was coupled up. It wasn't the season for romance, and yet it seemed to be blossoming all over the place. Maybe I was just being more sensitive than I should have been.

Maybe for the first time, I was feeling a little lonely.

I was jostled out of my thoughts when the taxi pulled to a halt. I fished around in my purse for the cash to pay the driver.

As I stepped out of the taxi, I noticed that the sidewalk was packed with people. They were all walking quickly, as if they had somewhere very important to be.

Today, I had somewhere important to be also.

I smiled as I headed inside the building with the best attitude I could muster. I was determined that I was going to have a great time and that I would be one of the star students.

How hard could it be?

THREE

I could smell the food cooking before I even pushed open the door.

Inside, there were students assembled at various counters. There was a central stove with many burners, as well as multiple ovens. It was easy to see that several of the students were couples. There were also a few single ladies.

I hoped I would fit in.

I tried to make my entrance subtle, but my purse caught on the handle of the door, causing the door to slam shut behind me.

All the students turned to look at me, as well as the teacher—the teacher who could have been carved out of perfection. He had the kind of chiseled chin and big bedroom eyes that melted my heart at first glance. His light brown hair was curly and hung against the back of his neck. The white apron he wore covered a strong frame.

"Welcome, everyone," he said, and I sighed with pleasure.

His Italian accent was rich and enticing. "Tonight we are here to learn, not just about cooking, but about passion." He smiled at each of the students, but it felt like he smiled just a little wider at me. I was really looking forward to listening to his voice all evening and was quite sure that I'd be fine with him teaching me anything about passion.

"First, we're going to start with getting things nice and hot," he said.

I was still staring at him when he walked over to me.

"Samantha, isn't it?"

I nodded slowly, not trusting myself to speak.

"Would you take it off for me?" he asked.

My eyes widened. My first instinct was to say yes—of course—where should I start? But I had a sneaking suspicion I was missing something.

I glanced around the room and saw that the other students were taking large pots down off the shelves above their stoves.

I felt my face get warm as I reached up to grab the pot. When I turned back to apologize, he had already walked away to the next student.

As he led us through the first step of filling the pot with the right amount of water, I tried to focus on the task at hand rather than the beautiful voice tantalizing my ears. I placed the pot on a burner and turned the temperature up to high. I was sure that I could at least handle boiling water, so I allowed my mind to drift off into a daydream of Vincenzo in nothing but an apron.

It was harmless to imagine such things.

"Samantha," he called to me. "It's too hot."

"Hm?" I asked, still a bit dazed by my fantasy.

"Samantha, turn it down or your water will boil over!"

Only then did I look back at the pot on my stove. The water was seeping out at the edge of the lid. The steam rose in large billows.

I cringed as the handle on the metal pan lid singed my skin. I had forgotten to pick up the potholder that lay so obvious in front of me.

I dropped the pan lid. It clattered against the floor, drawing the attention of all the students. They were looking directly at me when I reached down to pick up the lid and nearly tipped the whole boiling pot of water off the burner when I struck it with my elbow.

"Careful!" Vincenzo shouted and lunged forward to catch the pot before it could tilt enough to fall.

Of course he had the presence of mind to use the potholder that he had in his hand.

I straightened up with the pan lid in my hand and saw the look of fear in his eyes.

"Samantha, that is terribly dangerous," he said, his thick accent making his words sound delicious. But I was too embarrassed to enjoy them.

"I'm sorry." I couldn't look at him. "I don't know what's gotten into me. I just lost focus."

"Just take a breath, darling," Vincenzo said in the most soothing voice I'd ever heard. He ran his hand gently across my shoulders. His touch calmed me some. "Cooking should never be forced. It's something that has to flow out of you—

like speech—like love—like inspiration." He smiled and nodded as if he expected me to fully understand his words.

"Like inspiration," I repeated and nodded as if I understood.

But I didn't feel inspired. I felt embarrassed. That seemed to be my usual state these days. It seemed like everything I tried to accomplish turned into at least a small disaster, if not an epic one.

Vincenzo adjusted the temperature of the burner. Then he stirred my water so that it wouldn't froth over the top of the pot.

I felt miserable as I realized that so far the cooking class had only proven that I could not even, in fact, boil water.

I felt warm strong hands roll across my shoulders. The sudden touch was so relaxing that I closed my eyes for a moment to savor it. I opened my eyes again to see Vincenzo smiling at me.

"You're much too tense to cook. You must enjoy yourself, Samantha," he said. Then he handed me the garlic to add to the boiling water.

I nodded and managed a smile in return. At least most of the students were polite enough not to laugh at my expense, though I could tell from their averted gazes that they were embarrassed for me.

I focused on my pot of water. I sprinkled garlic in it until I could smell the flavor drifting up in the steam. As we moved on to the next step in the recipe, I could hear the passion in Vincenzo's voice.

"You must understand that when you are cooking a delicious meal, each and every ingredient is terribly important—even the dash of salt in the water—the diced onions added into the sauce. If you want to create a masterpiece then you must treat each and every ingredient as a piece of artwork, to be cherished by the tongue."

FOUR

My heart beat a little faster at his words. I met his eyes accidentally and he smiled warmly at me.

I liked the way he talked, not just because of his accent, but because of the passion he possessed. I didn't think there was anything in my life that I had ever been that passionate about. It was passion beyond a favorite hobby, it was a passion as if he'd stop breathing if he couldn't cook.

I wanted to feel that kind of passion as well.

I looked back at the ingredients, determined to follow his instructions. I sliced the tomatoes carefully. I simmered them in the olive oil and took extra care not to burn them. I added the diced onions exactly when he said to, despite the tears they brought to my eyes. Then I began to casually stir the mixture with my spatula.

My mind drifted as I watched the olive oil crackle in the pan. I thought of the man that I might make this meal for.

Would it be Max? Or would it be someone else entirely?

Was there really and truly one special person out there for me? Someone who could feel as passionate about me as—

"Samantha!"

Only then did I realize that the crackling had turned into a smoldering. I'd left the potholder too close to the burner. I had let the onions and tomatoes burn to a crisp, and now the potholder was beginning to smoke.

"Stand back!" Vincenzo shouted as he grabbed a small fire extinguisher and raced over to me.

"It's no big deal," I said, waving at the smoke like I was hosting a cooking show. "Just a little dramatic flair." I tossed a small amount of water onto the pan. This drew screams and gasps from the other students. I didn't understand why until flames abruptly jumped up from the pan.

I screamed and jumped back.

Vincenzo was right there with the fire extinguisher. He sprayed it until he was certain that the fire was out.

When he turned to face me, I couldn't tell by the look on his face whether he was furious or concerned.

"Are you okay?" he asked as he stared at me. "Did you get burned?"

"No," I stammered out and lowered my eyes. "I'm fine." I sighed.

"Samantha, look at me," he said.

I reluctantly looked up and met his eyes. I expected him to toss me out of the class—to accuse me of being the worst student he'd ever had.

"Never, ever, put water on a grease fire," he said with authority. "Understand?"

"Yes," I said. I was beyond embarrassed and could tell by

the heat I felt in my face that my cheeks had to be a bright shade of red by now. I could hear disdainful whispers from the other students. "I'm so sorry," I added and shook my head. "This obviously isn't the class for me. I should go." I grabbed my purse and turned to walk out of the kitchen.

Vincenzo grabbed me by the crook of my elbow. "Wait just a moment," he said. "I want to speak with you."

He turned back to the other students. "We're going to dismiss class early today. This class will not count towards your tuition. We will repeat the class and extend the sessions." He smiled apologetically to each of the students. "Please be sure that your stoves are fully off," he added.

The other students didn't seem overly pleased, but a few were coughing from the smoke in the air.

I couldn't look at them as they paraded past me one by one out the door. I felt so foolish. How did I get to be thirty-two years old without knowing the proper way to put out a fire?

Vincenzo's hand was still on my arm. I knew that if I pulled away he would let me go, but I was sure that he wanted to talk to me about the damage that had been done.

Once the last student was out the door, I turned to look at him. "I'm so sorry about the fire. I'll pay whatever extra I need to—to cover the damage."

"That's not why I asked you to stay, Samantha," he said as he turned to face me.

"It isn't?" I asked as I searched his eyes. "Then why did you?"

"I want to work with you—one-on-one." He was staring at me intently as he spoke.

"Oh, well, I can't really afford private lessons," I said with a slight shake of my head.

"No charge," he said.

I stared at him with disbelief. I couldn't imagine a professional chef giving his personal time to a hopeless student.

"Why?" I asked, mystified.

"Because, Samantha, I can see all of this passion bubbling inside of you." His hand drifted down from my elbow to my hand. "With no way to get out."

"I don't think cooking is the way." I laughed, feeling nervous.

"Oh, I think it can be," Vincenzo said. "You are in truth a fantastic cook, Samantha."

"Ha, I beg to differ," I laughed and looked at him with doubts filling my mind. I was trying to figure out if he was attempting to trick me for some reason.

"Differ all you want," he said as he gave my hand a light squeeze. "But I am right and you are wrong. I intend to show you—if you'll let me."

I loved the feeling of his touch. It was warm and strong, as if his fingertips had been trained to be tender. Maybe it was because I had been alone for so long, or maybe it was because he was being so kind to me, but I craved his attention after I'd felt that touch.

"Okay." I smiled. "Show me."

"Yes," he said squeezing my hand again before releasing it.

FIVE

Chef Vincenzo turned back to the stove I'd been working on. He tidied up the mess I had made, then he led me to another stovetop to use.

"You have the intelligence, the passion, and the creativity to be a great cook," he said as I followed him over to the new stove. "But there is one thing bottling all of that up."

"There is?" I asked. "What do you think it is?" I frowned.

"Tension."

The word rolled off his tongue as if it was a piece of art itself. I felt his voice travel through my body, as if he was strumming me from the inside.

"Tension?" I repeated.

"You can't relax," he said and slid a hand slowly along the top of my shoulders. "You hold yourself so tightly, like you're afraid that if you let go, you'll fall apart."

I could feel my face grow warm as I met his eyes. I felt as if he was seeing deeper into me than anyone had in some time.

"That's no way to live, Samantha," he whispered. "Life is about risk, about being willing to lose everything just so that you can truly experience what it is to be alive."

At some point my mind had drifted. I was sure of it, because his words faded and I could only see his lips moving sensuously around each word. My body was coming alive in a way that it hadn't in some time. I wanted to feel desirable and delicious, and the way he was looking at me, made me feel that way.

"Like this," he said.

The heat of his palm gliding along the back of my hand as he slowly stirred the sauce was more intense than the scent of the roasted garlic. I took a deep breath and felt a wave of lust, both for the meal we were cooking and the teacher who was guiding me. I was a little startled by it, as I didn't expect that I would be so enraptured by him.

"Slowly," he whispered beside my ear. "It's more of a swirl than a stir." I could sense his hips moving in a swirling motion. This of course meant that he was swirling against me, which made me swirl right back. "Perfect," he said, and I felt the tickle of his breath along my cheek. It was as spicy as the meal we were cooking, and it made my mouth water with the desire to taste both his lips and the dish. "Samantha," he said softly. "We're done with this part now."

I froze. I hoped I hadn't continued to swirl for as long as I thought I had. If I had, Vincenzo didn't seem to mind.

He lifted the spoon from the pot and then rested it on the counter beside the stove. I waited for him to step away, to create some space between us, but he didn't. He remained just as close to me.

"It's not just about the scent," he said, still standing next to me. "It's about the flavor, the taste, and the feeling that you have when you cook. It should be..." He paused a moment as if he was searching for the word.

"Sensual?" I said as I turned to look over my shoulder at him.

"Exactly." He smiled slowly as he met my eyes. "Sensual," he repeated and made my knees weak with just the word.

I felt as if I was trapped inside some lurid romance novel, at most of which I typically turned up my nose. Who had any of those kinds of experiences in real life? It certainly wasn't me.

Yet here I was, practically being seduced by a man whom I'd only just met.

"I can feel that," I said, my heart pounding.

"Does it feel hot?" he asked and moved even closer to me. His hand drifted around behind my back.

"So hot," I breathed out.

"You might be on fire," he said and grabbed me tight around the waist.

"Oh, I am definitely on fire!" I cried out and leaned upward, expecting him to kiss me.

Instead, he twirled me around and away from the stove.

"The burner–I think it might have singed your hair," he said with a frown as he stared at me.

My eyes widened. I realized I had yet again made a complete fool of myself.

In three sudden and determined strides he had me in his arms again. He kissed me without waiting for permission.

I felt electricity course along my spine, through every nerve in my body, until I was certain that I would boil over with passion.

When he pulled back and looked into my eyes I could see the same heat reflected in his gaze.

"I must have you, Samantha," he said with a flourish.

I tried not to crack a smile at his words. They were so steamy—so unexpected—but cheesy at the same time.

"But the meal—" I began to say.

He spun around quickly and turned everything off on the stove.

"Never mind that," he said as he turned back to me. "I want to cook for you. Take me home and I will cook for you there."

"Oh, I bet you will," I said in what I hoped was a sexy voice.

He nodded eagerly.

I licked my lips. I could taste the sauce on them still.

It had been so very long since I'd brought any man home to my apartment. I hadn't even been on a date with this man and yet I was fully considering inviting him into my bed. Heck, I wasn't considering, I was determined. In the past, I would have lectured any friend of mine that did the same. "The danger of casual sex," I recalled saying, "is far greater than the pleasure."

But I had been wrong. Vincenzo—whose last name I didn't even know—had a passion burning in his eyes that I wanted to feel too. I wanted him to awaken it in me.

'Yes," I gulped out. "Come home with me."

"Yes," he smiled and kissed me hard once more.

If I hadn't wanted to retain some level of dignity, I might have decided that going back to my place was going to take too long.

"We'll take my car," he said and grabbed his keys from the counter.

I blinked. I stared at him, as he looked at me expectantly.

"Samantha?" he asked as he gave me a puzzled look. "I asked if you would like a ride home?"

I felt deep disappointment as I realized fantasy and reality had merged. Vincenzo was offering me a lift, not a night of passionate lovemaking. I tried to keep from laughing as I thought about how quickly my imagination could take over.

I smiled. "Thank you."

It might not have been the seductive scene I had been imagining, but it was a start.

I had entered the cooking class certain that I would learn something about spice and flavor, and I was leaving with the same determination.

SIX

The ride to my apartment was filled with sexual tension—at least I thought it was. Vincenzo was impossible to read, as he was babbling on about sauces and the perfect firmness of pasta. I was just enjoying the sound of his voice.

When he parked at my apartment complex, I willed myself to kiss him—to ask him out on a date, to do anything that could possibly lead to the fantasy I'd had back in the classroom. But it was so much easier to just keep my mouth shut. It was so much less risky—so much safer not to put myself out there.

"Thanks," I said as I stepped out of the car.

When I closed the door behind me, Vincenzo was rounding the front of the car.

"I'll walk you," he said as he glanced around the dark parking lot. "It's late."

I smiled. "Don't worry, it's a safe area."

"I'll walk you," he said again and slipped his arm through mine.

I enjoyed him being so close to me.

We walked silently up to the door of my apartment. When we paused in front of it, he made no motion to leave. Instead, he gazed deeply into my eyes, as if he was waiting.

I stared at him intently. I could feel the words forming in my mind. I couldn't believe that I was really going to ask. But I couldn't stop myself from speaking.

"Do you want to come inside?" I asked and giggled. Yes, I giggled.

Vincenzo smiled. "I would love to," he said with a nod and took my hand gently in his own.

I smiled and turned the key in the lock. I felt my heart racing. This was a big no-no on my list of things that I, Samantha Bradford, did *not* do.

If a man wanted to see the inside of my apartment, he had to take me out on at least three dates, and that was only to stand inside the door while I grabbed my coat. But I had already invited him in; there was no turning back now. It would be rude.

I pushed the door open.

Vincenzo stepped in after me.

I was being brave, I told myself. I was being very brave.

"Sorry, it's a bit of a mess." I cringed as I noticed some of my clothes and a towel draped over various pieces of furniture.

"It's just fine," Vincenzo said. "Remember, Samantha, you must relax." He reached out and began rubbing my shoulders.

"Oh, um," I whispered, feeling very flustered. "Can I get you a drink?"

"Sure." I felt his lips brush along the curve of my neck as he spoke.

I slipped away from him and headed into the kitchen.

All of a sudden my heart was hammering for another reason. I had just invited a complete stranger into my home. He was already nuzzling my neck. I didn't even know if Vincenzo was his last name or his first name. I shuddered as I grabbed a bottle of wine. I wanted to be this love-on-a-whim type of woman, but I wasn't very good at it.

I could see the headlines in the newspaper:

Desperate young woman invites a stranger into her room and no one is surprised when she's found chopped into bits.

"Samantha?" Vincenzo called out from the living room. "Do you need some help?"

I was so startled by the sound of his voice that the bottle of wine slipped out of my hand. It shattered against the floor, spilling shards of glass and puddles of red wine. It looked like a crime scene had materialized.

"I'll be right there."

"Samantha?" he said again, only this time he was standing right inside my kitchen. "What happened?" I was on my knees trying to gather the shards of glass together. "No, no," he said. "Don't do that, you might—"

"Ouch," I cursed under my breath—the red that was spreading across my palm was not wine. "I'm sorry," I said as I looked up at him. I was on my knees in the middle of a huge mess, and to top it off, I was now bleeding. What he must have thought as he looked at me, I didn't even want to imagine.

He snatched a towel off the oven door handle and crouched down in front of me.

"Shh... accidents happen." He reached for my hand.

I spread my fingers out. He pressed the towel gently against the cut in my palm. It was just a thin slice, but it felt good to have someone tend to my wounds.

"To me, they seem to happen all the time." I sighed and gazed into his beautiful brown eyes.

Only moments before, I had been imagining that this man could be a killer. Now he was being so tender that I was certain I had lost my mind.

"Don't worry so much, Samantha, and then you won't have so many accidents." He chuckled and pulled the towel away. "See? All better."

I smiled at him and took the towel. I remembered why I had invited him in. He had a very honest nature. I grabbed a dustpan and broom to get the rest of the glass picked up.

"There's another bottle of wine in the refrigerator," I said as I scooped up the glass.

"Oh, Samantha," he said as he surveyed the contents of my refrigerator, "I will have to take you shopping."

I laughed a little at that and washed my hands carefully in the sink.

By the time I turned around he had already poured us both a glass of wine.

"To a passionate evening," he said as he offered me my glass. I reached for it, but he tugged it back playfully. "Relax, Samantha, or you might drop it."

I smiled, feeling shy as I took the glass in my hand. "Thank you."

"You're welcome." He sipped his wine.

SEVEN

As Vincenzo and I walked back into the living room, I still felt a little uneasy. Bringing someone into my apartment was like bringing them into my psyche. So much could be learned about me if one knew where to look.

"This is a nice place you have here," he said and sat down on the sofa.

I sat down beside him.

"It does the job." I laughed.

"Have you lived here long?"

"For quite some time." I didn't want him to think that I was strange for living in the same apartment for nearly ten years.

"Well, then it is home," he said and sipped his wine again.

I felt his arm drift over my shoulders. Instantly, I tensed up. So did my grasp on the stem of the wine glass. I nearly spilled some with the sudden jerk of my hand. I reminded myself to relax. It was just a glass of wine—just a lovely evening between friends—and it didn't have to lead to anything more than that, except—oh my god, that was his lips on my neck.

Vincenzo had put his glass down on the table beside the sofa. His lips were nuzzling playfully at the sensitive curve of my neck. I would have protested, if I weren't already drifting into pleasure.

I felt him take the wine from my hand. He set it down carefully. Then he kissed me. It was a kiss that was much more than a kiss. It was a kiss of passion, of lust, of fireworks.

With a shiver I pulled back slightly from him.

"Vincenzo, this is a little fast for me."

"It is as fast as passion is dictating," he said.

I narrowed my eyes. Pretty words never convinced me of anything. But the glide of his hand along my thigh...

"I don't normally do this," I breathed out.

He kissed me again. I began to feel my body unwind. Be brave, Samantha, it was pleading.

"Just relax," Vincenzo whispered as he slipped his arms around me. "Sometimes the body must have what it must have."

His words sank in as my mind spun with desire. It really wasn't something I would normally do. But I felt as if there was no turning back. As Vincenzo had said, sometimes the body must have what it must have.

The thing about unplanned sleepovers is that you never think about having company in your bedroom when you leave your panties in a ball on the floor, or used tissues in a pile, or your teddy bear staring down from a shelf that overlooks your bed. All of those things seem perfectly normal when you leave your bedroom in the morning—but not when you return with Vincenzo on your arm.

I turned off the light as soon as we walked into the room, hoping to hide most of my transgressions.

Vincenzo didn't seem to care. Instead, he spent quite some time, teaching me just how to relax.

By the time we were snuggled close in the afterglow, I felt more relaxed than I could recall ever feeling. In that span of time, Max didn't even cross my mind. The dirty tissues in a pile ceased to exist. The glaringly obvious risk of having a stranger in my bed seemed completely unimportant.

All that mattered was Vincenzo's arms around me.

"Marry me, my love." He kissed softly along the back of my neck.

"What?"

"I didn't say anything," he murmured and continued to kiss me.

Of course he hadn't. That had been my imagination skipping straight past second date and into matching bath towels.

My mind drifted to what our babies would look like, what our home would be like, what our wedding would be like.

"Vincenzo," I whispered and turned toward him, only to find that he was snoring softly.

I smiled at his sweet slumbering face. It was a face I could get used to waking up next to.

I snuggled close to him and closed my eyes.

I was very relieved that he wasn't a serial killer. My standards were evolving.

In my dreams, I could see my life unfolding. There was a man beside me, as I bought a house, as I had a child, as I began to grow old. It was a lovely dream.

But every time I turned to look at the man of my dreams, he seemed to be turning away. I could never see more than a glimpse of the back of his head.

When I opened my eyes, I was smiling.

I rolled over in the bed to find Vincenzo right beside me. He was still sound asleep, his breathing heavy. He gasped a little when he snored. The bed was so warm, I almost didn't want to get out. But I wanted to surprise him with what I could do when I was relaxed.

I pulled on a long t-shirt and wandered out into the kitchen.

Once the coffee was going, I set about creating a delicious breakfast.

I was excited to prepare breakfast for Vincenzo. I knew it would be nothing compared to what he could create, but I was looking forward to showing him that I was trying.

I gathered the things I needed from my small pantry, tucked my ear buds into my ears, and turned the music up loud. I danced around the kitchen as I tossed in the ingredients.

I couldn't hear the sizzle of the oil, but I could smell the scent of the seasoning. It was making my mouth water.

As I continued to dance, I thought about how easily my body moved. I remembered my pole dancing class and how

I'd shifted into another state of mind while I'd danced. I couldn't even remember what I'd done, but whatever it was had drawn admiration from the other students.

I felt like I was right on the edge of that other state of mind once more.

EIGHT

I felt a hand on my hip.

I smiled, thinking that Vincenzo had slipped out of bed and sneaked up on me. His touch reminded me to relax. I closed my eyes and our bodies swayed together. I made sure that my movements were as sensual as they had been the night before, as he had seemed to enjoy them then.

In the midst of our dancing the ear buds popped out of my ears.

"That smells so good," he whispered in my ear and pulled my body close against his. "Is it for me?"

My eyes popped open. My mouth dropped open and my stomach fluttered with arousal and anxiety. It wasn't Vincenzo that had been dancing with me at all.

It was Max.

Of course it was Max. Because my life refuses to unfold in a calm, orderly fashion.

"Max!" I shoved him away from me.

He looked confused and a little hurt. "I'm sorry, I really

enjoyed the dance," he sputtered out. "I didn't mean to upset you."

"I just didn't know it was you!"

"Huh?" Max looked terribly confused. "Who else could it be? I'm the only one with a key and we always have breakfast on Saturday morning." He frowned.

"Oh, Max." I sighed as I realized he was right. I remembered Vincenzo curled up in my bed and put my finger to my lips. "You have to go," I whispered and tried to push him toward the door. "Please, you have to go right now."

"Why?" He shook his head and refused to be moved. "I don't understand what the problem is."

"Please, Max. I'll tell you later. Just leave." I tried to usher him toward the door once more.

"Is this another one of those ploys to keep me on my toes?" he asked, looking as frustrated as I felt. "Really, Sam, if you didn't want me to come today, all you had to do was tell me." He shook his head and turned toward the door.

"It's not that, Max, please." I groaned as I realized I was really upsetting him. "It's just that I'm not alone—" I began to explain. Before I could finish getting the words out, another voice spoke over mine.

"Samantha." Vincenzo's rich voice called out from my bedroom. "Something is burning!"

Max's eyes widened as he realized what was happening. But I didn't have time to explain, because Vincenzo was right, something was burning.

"Oh!" I turned toward the stove, where a plume of smoke had begun forming.

"Sam, you should have just told me," Max said. "You

have someone here." He shook his head, his face flushed. "How could I be so stupid? Is this all to make me jealous or something?"

I was too focused on the smoke to pay much attention to his words.

I grabbed the pan by the handle, causing my palm to burn. I cursed as I dropped it and spilled half of its blackened contents across the stove.

"Samantha, are you alright?" Vincenzo called out, and I could tell from the sound of his voice that he was heading out into the kitchen. I began to panic. If Vincenzo saw Max —if Max saw Vincenzo—these things could only happen to me!

"Max, please," I said as I turned to face him with desperation. "Just go."

He stared at me for a long moment, as if he was deciding what he really wanted to do. Then he cast a glare in the direction of my bedroom.

For an instant, I thought he might decide to confront Vincenzo.

He turned and walked out of the apartment, and he wasn't very quiet about closing the door behind him.

"Oh, Samantha," Vincenzo said as he looked over the remainder of the breakfast I had been preparing. "You shouldn't have, really."

"I know," I sighed as I leaned back against the sink.

I was staring at the door. What had Max meant by making him jealous? Had he meant what I thought he meant? Did it really bother him to see me with another man? If so, what did that mean?

"Here, I'll make us something," Vincenzo said as he tossed the pan into the sink.

"No, actually." My voice wavered. "I think maybe you should go."

"Go?" he asked and lifted an eyebrow. "Have I done something to upset you?"

"No, of course not. You were *great*," I said and emphasized the last word. It was true; I was still tingling with the memories of what we had shared. "I just forgot that I had plans this morning. You know, we got caught up in the heat of the moment last night—"

"I want it to be more than just a moment, Samantha," he said and stepped close to me. "Don't you?" He met my eyes intently.

I didn't know what to say. This morning I had been visualizing our future—opening a restaurant together, having beautiful babies with accents, eating delicious meals every single night.

But then—there was Max.

Max, who looked as if he wanted to burn my apartment down because there was another man sleeping in my bed. Max, whom I had been longing to be with for over ten years, whom I had finally lost all hope of being with.

I needed to know what he meant. I needed to know if there was a chance for us.

"I'm sorry, Vincenzo." I shook my head. "I'm just not really available for a relationship right now."

"You're with someone?" he asked, sounding surprised.

"No—It's not like that. I just—"

"I understand." Vincenzo nodded before I could continue. "I'll just get my things."

As I watched him walk back into the bedroom, I wondered if I should follow him in—if I should plead for his forgiveness, if I should give whatever spark was between us a chance.

When he stepped back out, he met my eyes directly. "Just so you know, I don't normally do this either," he said, not looking at all pleased. Then he pushed past me and out the door of my apartment.

As it closed behind him, I realized I didn't even have his phone number. I certainly couldn't go back to his class.

I rushed into my room and threw on some clothes.

I knew exactly where Max would be going.

NINE

I must have looked like a lunatic as I ran down the sidewalk after Max. But I didn't care. I wanted an explanation for the way he had behaved at my apartment.

"Max!" I called out as he continued to walk down the street.

I ran fast until I caught up with him. He shoved his hands deep into his pockets and refused to stop walking. "Max, what in the world do you have to be mad at me about?" I said, feeling completely frustrated and confused. "Because I had a man in my apartment?"

"You just should have let me know," Max said with an edge to his voice. "I wouldn't have walked into the middle of that if I had known what was going on."

"I forgot," I said. "I got caught up with Vincenzo. It was so sudden and—"

"Vincenzo," he said and finally stopped walking to look at me. "I bet that isn't even his real name."

"Why would you say that?" I asked.

"Don't you get it? That type of guy sets himself up as a teacher so he can get women to sleep with him." He shook his head.

"No, that's not true. Vincenzo wanted more than that—he told me so."

"And?" Max asked as he rocked back on his heels and studied me. "What about you? Is that what you want?"

Everything in my body, my mind, and my heart wanted me to scream out that it was him I wanted, but I was still feeling nervous about revealing the truth.

"Max, what did you mean when you said I was trying to make you jealous?" I asked as I held his gaze and my breath.

"By bringing a man home—by not canceling breakfast with me," he muttered and frowned. "I don't get what you're asking."

"I'm asking, why would you be jealous?" I stared deep into his eyes. I waited for some sign that he was going to confess to having feelings for me.

But he flicked his gaze away and looked down the block. He pursed his lips and then slowly relaxed as he turned back to look at me. "You know, Sammy, I shouldn't be jealous," he said. "You have every right to be happy. You deserve to be happy."

I felt my heart begin to race. He was about to say the words I had expected he would—that I'd dreamed he would.

"Max—" I started to confess my own feelings, but the words stuck in my throat.

He turned to look at me again. I felt his palm glide along the curve of my cheek as he met my eyes.

"I'm sorry, Sam," he whispered. "I had no right to get

upset. I'm sure you just forgot about me in the heat of the moment. That's okay."

I swallowed thickly and willed myself not to allow tears to form. I felt as if he was crushing me once more. I had really believed that this time he would see it—he would see that we were meant to be together—that we had always been meant to be together.

"Yes," I said finally. "I just forgot."

"It's fine," he shrugged. "You should get back to Vincenzo."

"He's gone," I whispered.

"Oh." He nodded a little. "I hope not because of me. I can explain to him that we're just friends, if you want."

"No. Don't worry about it."

"Well, in that case, do you want to grab some breakfast?"

"I don't think so," I mumbled and turned away from him.

I felt his eyes on me as I walked away.

I kept hoping that he would call out to me, that he would declare that he was in love with me—that I hadn't just rejected an amazing, passionate man, for one who would only ever see me as a friend.

In the span of one day, I'd gone from the depths of loneliness to the height of passion—and right back to loneliness again. I felt like an idiot.

I knew that if I stayed at home, all I would think about would be Vincenzo, so I headed to work to cover a shift. Fluff and Stuff had become a place of refuge for me.

I could always think more clearly with the whir of laundry machines around me.

TEN

The swirl of the washer was a little relaxing, but not enough for me to forget what I had done. My mind kept drifting back to Vincenzo.

Vincenzo, with the lovely voice and the amazing touch. Vincenzo, who was the first man I had let near me since my last real relationship. It was so unlike me to bring someone back to my place to spend the night. But it had happened.

I didn't regret sleeping with Vincenzo, but I did regret the way I had treated him. If the roles had been reversed, I would have been devastated.

Maybe Max was right. Maybe Vincenzo really did only teach the class so that he could get women. It had certainly worked with me. But either way, he had chosen to share that intimacy with me, and instead of honoring that, I had tossed him aside at the first hint of Max's attention. Yet again, I was allowing our years of history to interfere with my daily life.

It was hard not to, when it seemed as if every time I was ready to give up, Max managed to toss me a crumb.

"Why so glum, chum?" a voice chimed out as a woman walked into the laundromat.

"Hi, Bee," I said, still feeling sad as I continued to listen to the swirl of the washer.

"I didn't think that you were working today," Bee said with a slight frown.

She had a big laundry basket filled with mostly red shirts and jeans. Bee liked very specific things. She liked her food a certain way, only certain colors of clothing, and only one washer and dryer. She always wore her hair in a snug braid pinned to the base of her head. She never wandered from her routines.

"I wasn't," I said as I walked over to the washer that I knew she would want to use. I checked to make sure there was nothing lingering in it and then tossed in a few quarters to start the water flowing. "But I decided to come in and cover a shift."

"Well, that was nice of you," she said with a laugh. She shook out each shirt carefully before tossing it into the water. "But why are you *really* here?"

"I had nowhere better to be," I admitted and slumped down beside the washer once more.

"Is this about Max?" Bee asked with an arched eyebrow.

"Huh?"

"Oh, please, don't even try to deny it," Bee said with a smile on her dark-red lips. "It's written all over your face every time you see him."

"It is?" I asked and touched my cheek lightly. "I didn't think it showed."

"Well, maybe not to everybody." Bee shrugged. "But I'm

not just anybody. I notice things that others don't. I notice that you are always smiling when Max is around."

"Not any more," I said, not bothering to hide my annoyance. "That guy drives me nuts."

"Mm-hm," Bee said and snapped one of her shirts sharply.

"He does," I insisted. "He's with a different woman all the time. He finds something wrong with everyone he dates. He expects everyone to be perfect!"

"Oh, dear." Bee shook her head as she closed the lid on her washer. "I think you're in deeper than you realize."

"What do you mean? He's the one with the problem."

"He may be picky." Bee nodded. "I mean, I have noticed that he is always with a certain type of girl. But I know a little something about needing things to be perfect. Do you think I *want* to wear only red?"

"Well, I assumed so," I said with a frown.

"No, I'd love to wear any other color," she said and then walked over to me. "I have a need for things to be in a certain order. Things in my life must always be done a certain way. But I have no real choice in the matter. It's a compulsion, and I can't control it. Everything must be perfect." She sighed. "When I see other people seeking perfection, waiting for things to be just right, I want to shout at them to just be messy. When you get caught up in perfect, it owns you. It steals your entire life from you."

I gazed into her deep brown eyes. I could see the mixture of pain and honesty there.

"I hear you, Bee," I said softly.

"Do, my dear," she said and turned back to her washer. "Because life is so much sweeter when it's messy."

I glanced around the laundromat. Considering my track record with fire and wine bottles, I was apparently well on my way to sweetness.

That night when I settled in front of my computer to create my blog post I felt so many different things. Elation over the night I had spent with Vincenzo, regret over the night I had spent with Vincenzo. Anger at Max, longing for Max. But most of all, I felt Bee's advice.

I typed quickly on the keyboard. I titled my blog post:

Learning to Relax and Be Messy

As I revealed my experiences with the cooking class, Vincenzo, and Bee, I felt all of the pieces falling into place for me. My life hadn't stalled; I had forced it to stop. I had been treading water for years, fearing the possibility that I might drown, when, in fact, I'd been able to swim the whole time.

I posted my blog and sat back in my chair. I was about to close my computer, when a ping announced that I had a new comment.

It was from Blue. I was surprised that I had a response so quickly.

Amazing words as always. SWF, I hope that you get to be as messy as you please. Everyone deserves a life of passion.

I stared at the words for a moment. Blue was the only person that had been commenting on my blog so far. It was quite mysterious to me that a complete stranger could be so interested in my life. But it was also inspiring.

Yes, I needed more passion in my life. But I needed a real outlet for it. I needed new perspective and creativity. I needed to not just experience my life, but visualize and create it.

Hopefully the next item on my bucket list would help me with that.

#4 CREATE A MASTERPIECE

ONE

I believe creativity is a very big part of living passionately. Being able to express yourself on paper, on canvas, or even through needle and thread puts a little of yourself out into the universe. It lets you leave a mark in a world that might otherwise never notice you. So, I was determined to participate in a little creativity.

Lately, because of my blog, I had discovered a love of writing. But I had always wanted to be an artist. As a child I attempted drawing quite a few times, but the results were stick figures and flowers that looked like balloons. I put my childish dreams away along with my crayons and markers.

Something had sparked me to try again. As I was struggling to sketch an image of a bird, I wondered how it could come so easily for some and why it was so difficult for others. Then I thought about the new experiences that I'd had in the past few weeks.

Pole dancing class, cooking class—all of those things had led me to a new perspective on life.

Maybe taking an art class would help me explore my desire to create on canvas. It was on my bucket list to create a masterpiece. I wasn't sure that a class could help me with that, but I was willing to find out.

I looked up local classes and found a painting class that met on Tuesday and Thursday evenings. I decided that this would be a good option for me. I called to sign up and managed to land the last spot.

"Must be a fun class," I muttered to myself as I hung up the phone. I smiled as I realized that I would be marking off yet another item on my list. I couldn't wait for the class to start. Especially since the bird I had been sketching all morning looked more like a marshmallow with growths.

I checked my watch and discovered it was time to head into Fluff and Stuff. As the manager, I took my role there very seriously. I was almost never late. Since it was a few blocks from my apartment, I didn't have far to go.

I grabbed my sketchbook so that I could keep practicing if it was a slow day. I was already worried about whether I would be the worst student in the class.

As I walked up to the shop, I saw my friend Max was waiting for me outside the door.

"Morning, beautiful," he said as he smiled at me.

I smiled back, but tried to ignore the compliment.

"Morning. Don't you have to work today?" I asked as I unlocked the door and stepped inside.

He followed me in.

I flipped on the field of fluorescent lights that populated the ceiling above the assortment of washing machines and dryers.

"I did, but then I decided to take the morning off."

"Getting tired of fixing computers?" I asked, teasing him. "Ready to come back to the delightful scent of fabric softener?" I snatched up a gauzy dryer sheet and waved it under his nose.

"Ugh." He turned his head and sneezed. "No, absolutely not." He laughed and shook his head. "Also, I don't fix computers all day—you know that," he stated with some annoyance.

"Okay, okay." I shrugged. "Whatever it is that you do can't be more entertaining than this place."

Max leaned back against one of the dryers and watched as I went through and checked each of the washers for any wayward clothing. I had a tendency to be a little obsessive about the safety and cleanliness of the place.

"No, not more entertaining," he agreed. "Isn't it Old Joe's day?" He smiled.

I froze in front of the washers, and a feeling of dread filled me. Old Joe was not exactly the entertaining part of Fluff and Stuff.

He had been using the combination laundromat and shop since I'd begun working at the place in college. He always had an entire load of stinky grungy socks. There were more socks than any man should ever own, and I could never figure out how he could possibly get them so dirty. He also made sure that every single item of clothing was folded as compact as possible. It wasn't about being wrinkle-free for Old Joe, it was about conserving space.

He usually paid for the full laundry service, which meant that it was up to me to whiten his socks and to minimize his laundry into tiny little balls of material. He wasn't a bad guy, but he had gotten quite a reputation for his laundry quirks.

"Yes. Yes, I guess it is," I said, attempting to hide how much I was dreading his arrival.

"Well, I guess that's one good thing about not working here anymore," Max said and laughed.

I looked up at him. He was so handsome when he laughed. His smile was fine, but when he laughed, his eyes crinkled, his cheeks pinked up, and his dimples were exposed. It was my favorite way to see him. I tried not to be distracted by the flutter of my heart.

"Well, I'm sure you have something better to do than hang out here if you have the morning off." I didn't realize the bite to my voice until after I'd spoken.

I think that Max must have noticed too.

He blinked once as if he had been struck by the words.

"I was hoping to take you to lunch," he said quietly, the amusement gone from his voice.

TWO

Things had been awkward between Max and me lately. I was trying to cure myself of a decade-old crush on the guy who was my best friend.

"I'm sorry, I'm covering the entire day shift," I said and tried not to notice the hurt in his eyes.

"Then I could bring something in."

"I don't think so. I'm trying to eat healthier," I reminded him. "I don't want to gain everything back."

"Alright, alright." He nodded a little. I could tell that he was annoyed. "It just seems like I haven't seen much of you lately." He sighed.

"I have been a little busier than usual."

The truth was that I had been doing my very best to avoid Max.

I loved him.

Not in a casual, "oh he's cute" way.

In an inconvenient, life-altering, please-make-it-stop kind of way.

"In fact, I have a class tonight," I added with a slight smile. "I think all those comments you've made about me being in the same job since college have made me realize that I need to expand my horizons a little."

"I never meant to hurt your feelings."

"You didn't. Not at all. In fact, you reminded me that there is a world outside of Fluff and Stuff. All these years I've been waiting to live, because I didn't think I had a right to be happy with all that extra fluff." I laughed a little at my joke. "Now I see how silly that was. I'm ready to enjoy the things that I've been avoiding."

"Well, I think that's a good thing," he said with a slight nod. "I just hope that you don't forget—you're beautiful, no matter what shape or size."

"I know, I know," I said, smiling at him.

Max had never once let me put myself down because of being overweight. Despite the fact that he dated women that could be models, he never teased me about my extra pounds. In fact, he had always done the opposite, taking every opportunity to compliment me. How could I not fall in love with a guy like that?

"I guess it's finally sinking in," I added.

"I'm glad that you're having so much fun," Max said. "Just don't forget about your partner in crime."

"I won't." I briefly met his eyes.

I felt that flutter again. I would never want to forget about Max entirely. We were so close that he felt like an extension of me, but I needed desperately to forget that pesky little flutter. At thirty-two I needed to be done waiting for him to feel it too.

"Why don't we get together tomorrow night?" I said. "We could go to that little casino that just opened. It has penny slots!"

"That sounds like fun." Max nodded. "But I have a date tomorrow night. She wants to go ballroom dancing." He rolled his eyes. "Whatever happened to just dinner and a movie?"

"You're a great dancer," I reminded him. "You should go and show off."

"I guess, but it seems like a lot of pressure for a first date."

"First date? What happened to Patti?"

"She was great." Max frowned. "But she wanted a commitment and we'd only been dating a few weeks. That's way too fast for me."

"You know, Max, you are getting older."

Max ran his hand back over his hair looking self-conscious, as if he was checking for a receding hairline.

"And?" he asked.

"And the women you date are going to be more interested in moving things along. What's so bad about a little commitment?"

"So, I'm just supposed to commit, even if I don't think the woman I'm with is a woman I want to commit to?"

"I don't think you've found any woman that you've wanted to commit to. Maybe if you gave it a try you'd discover that it's easier than you think."

"No way." Max shook his head. "I'm saving myself."

I blinked.

"For what?" I asked. "The apocalypse?"

"Not like that," he said and scowled. "I mean, I'm not

going to settle. I'm not going to get trapped into marriage and kids unless the woman I'm with blows my socks off."

"Trapped, eh?" I glanced at him out of the corner of my eye. "That attitude might be part of the problem."

"No, the problem is that there is no problem." Max smiled confidently. "It's normal to date around."

"Maybe." I shrugged and stepped into the shop area to make sure that all the items were arranged properly. The small shop connected to the laundromat had an assortment of items for sale—from candy to canned soup to souvenirs to one-of-a-kind yard sale finds.

Max followed after me. "You're one to talk," he said. "That chef was the first man I've seen you with—"

"Stop right there," I warned him with a sharp glare. "My love life is my business."

"Oh, I see." He chuckled. "So mine is fair game, but yours is a government secret."

"Seems that way," I said. "You'll have to tell me how the ballroom dancing goes."

"And you?" he asked. "What class are you taking tonight?"

"A painting class."

"Oh."

I could tell that he was trying not to laugh.

"What?" I said, not trying to contain my annoyance.

"Uh, well," he cleared his throat. "It's just I've seen some of your drawings and—"

"Max!" I shouted at him and picked up a loofah to throw at his head. "That's why I'm taking a class."

"Alright." He laughed. "If that's what you really want to do."

"It is," I said, feeling confident again. "You'll see. When I'm done, I'll have a masterpiece."

He stared at me for a long moment. "Honestly, Sammy, I wouldn't doubt that for a second. You have always been able to do anything you put your mind to."

I smiled at him. "Thanks, Max, that means a lot."

"Just don't forget about me when you become a famous artist. I'll leave you to your laundry." He gave me a quick hug.

A few customers had already walked in to use the washers and dryers. I could see that it wasn't likely to be a slow day.

"Thanks. And Max, give the slow dancing a chance," I said as I met his eyes. "Sometimes to get your socks blown off you have to be willing to slow down a little."

"Ha, ha." He nodded and walked out of the laundromat.

I watched him go for longer than I should have. That familiar longing rose within me. I squashed it down as I went about my work.

As I got into the swing of the day, I found myself thinking about the people that came in and out of the laundromat. I pictured them as portraits—as moments of pure art in the middle of the mundane.

I had a tendency to notice the minute beauty in things—the soft curve of someone's lips, the way the ridge of an ear angled in a unique way, even the weathered surface of the skin of Old Joe's fingers.

To me each of these things held a beauty that only that particular person possessed.

I wondered if that was something that I could ever capture on canvas. I hoped that it might be.

By the time I was closing up shop for the night, I was excited for my first painting class. Maybe I just needed a little guidance, and I would finally be able to create the beauty I witnessed each day.

THREE

When I walked into the classroom, the first thing I noticed was how large it was. There were at least fifteen easels set up, with students at all but one, which I assumed was mine. There was a large area at the front of the room where a woman, whom I assumed was the teacher, was pacing slowly back and forth. She had her eyes closed and her fingers steepled, as if she was saying a prayer. She was dressed in a long flowing white dress. Her long blonde hair had flowers intertwined.

I hadn't seen a grown woman with flowers in her hair since a music festival I'd attended purely for the nachos.

I paused in the doorway, wondering if I should go through with it. I could see some of the artwork hung on the walls, and none of it looked like a marshmallow with growths.

I felt a nervous knot in the pit of my stomach. I knew it was my familiar feeling of not being good enough. That feeling had stopped me doing so many things in life, from believing I could lose weight to believing that I could pursue any dream I had. I wasn't going to let it stop me doing this too.

I walked slowly into the classroom despite my fear.

"Hello." A woman at the easel beside me smiled. She looked friendly enough, with frizzy black hair that hung to her waist, and bright blue eyes. She had the kind of tan that came from working outside, not tanning. She was working on a painting—a landscape—and it was so realistic that I could have mistaken it easily for a photograph.

"Hello," I said. "I'm Samantha. Your painting is beautiful."

"Oh, thank you." She laughed, looking slightly embarrassed. "It has a lot of room for improvement. I'm Stephanie."

I hid my surprise at the idea that there was anything about the painting that could improve.

"Have you been taking the class long?" I asked as I sat down behind my easel.

"No, this is only my second night. I just love to paint."

I felt another wave of queasiness. I wondered if there was some sort of test I should have taken before starting the class to see if I was even capable of being a beginner.

"It's beautiful," I said again, feeling a little numb.

"Oh, good, everyone is here," the teacher said from the front of the room.

She had a soft voice. I had to strain a little to hear each word.

"I want to welcome everyone to this joyous evening," she said with a happy sigh.

I glanced over at Stephanie, who winked lightly at me.

"She's a little strange," she whispered. "But she's a great teacher."

I nodded and smiled, feeling relieved. At least I wasn't the only one to find her behavior a little odd.

"So in previous classes we have discussed sight. What is sight?" she asked as she walked back and forth in front of the class. "It's not just seeing, is it?"

I stared at her with disbelief. Then I looked over at Stephanie. Stephanie seemed to be enthralled by the teacher's words.

"What do you think, Samantha?" the teacher asked. I assumed she was singling me out because I was a new student. "Do you think that sight is just seeing?"

One of the most difficult things for me to deal with is being put on the spot with a question. My impulsive answers were usually nonsense and had nothing to do with the question. However, this question was so simple, I didn't hesitate to answer.

"Well, it is seeing," I said with confidence. "I mean, that is what sight is for."

"Oh dear." The teacher laughed. She walked up to me and knocked lightly on the top of my head, as if checking for available storage space. I wasn't sure whether to swat her or duck. "I think we're going to need to open you up a little bit." She smiled at me.

Her words were spoken in a kind voice, but I didn't think that she was being kind at all.

"I don't understand, I guess." I felt as if everyone was in on some secret that I was not privy to.

"When we see, it is not about just having sight," the

teacher explained as she walked back toward the front of the classroom. "It's about knowing what we see. We don't just look, we seek to understand, to define—don't we?" she asked.

I nodded a little. I could grasp the concept. I frowned and ducked behind my easel. I was a little annoyed that she had used me as an example of someone's mind being closed. I wanted more than anything to bring up all of the ways I had been opening myself up lately, but she was already well into her lecture.

"When it comes to painting, we can't just paint what we see. We must paint what we know—what we have come to understand," she said. "Today our subject is a bowl of fruit." She picked up a bowl from her desk. "As you can see, there are apples, bananas, oranges, grapes, plums, and a few strawberries." She set the bowl down on a small card table in the center of the front of the room. "Let's get started," she said with a smile and a clap of her hands.

FOUR

I stared at the fruit. Now, I had been dieting for over a year. So I had learned to appreciate all kinds of fruits and vegetables, but I had never really thought about painting them. It seemed a little silly to me to do so. They didn't have character to me like a person would.

Still, everyone else was happily painting them, so I decided to give it a shot.

I started with the bowl.

By the time I was done with it, it looked more like a square than a circle. It looked a little lopsided, and there wasn't any depth to it.

The teacher walked past me and paused. She looked at my version of the bowl for a moment and then tore the paper off my easel.

"Try again," she said. "Don't just look at the bowl—go inside the bowl, walk around the bowl—be the bowl." She smiled at me.

I had not emotionally prepared to become pottery that evening.

The sound of the paper tearing off the easel had drawn the attention of some of my classmates.

Stephanie's bowl looked like a bowl.

As the teacher walked away Stephanie leaned over and whispered to me. "She's all about feeling," she said. "Just keep trying, you'll get it. You have to give the bowl shape; it's not flat in real life—it can't be flat on your paper either."

I smiled at her to thank her, but I still wasn't sure if I understood. I had to give the bowl shape. It wasn't flat. It was round, and full, and curvy. I narrowed my eyes and tried to create the bowl with depth and character.

When I was done, it still didn't look like the bowl, but it certainly did look a lot better than my first attempt. I smiled proudly.

Stephanie nodded at me. She was already working on the banana.

As I drew the different fruits, I discovered that they were just as unique as the people I saw each day. Different textures, different shapes. It was relaxing to think about.

Soon I was drawing without even paying attention to whether I was drawing well or not. I was just drawing the fruit as I experienced it.

"Magnificent," the teacher said with approval as she walked past me.

I was startled out of the relaxed state I had settled into. I stared at the image on the paper in front of me. The fruit was a little off in size and the apple seemed to be hovering like it had spiritual aspirations, but I was surprised that it actually did look like fruit.

"It needs a lot of work," I said with a laugh.

"Oh, hon, a painting is never about what it needs," the teacher said gently. "It's always about what the artist needs."

I stared at her for a moment. I wasn't sure if she was nicely insulting me, but her words made sense. The painting was my perspective; it was how I saw the world around me, how I expressed it on paper. If I didn't like what I saw, then it wasn't the painting I needed to improve, it was my perspective.

I ripped off the paper myself and started over. I no longer thought about shape or size or the position of the fruit. Instead, I thought about the beauty of it. I didn't draw a circle, I drew an orange. I drew it as I recalled its scent. I drew it as I recalled its taste. I drew it as I recalled its texture beneath my fingertips. It wasn't about how it looked; it was about communicating what it actually was.

By the time I had finished the painting, I was stunned by what I'd created. Sure, it still wasn't flawless, but it was better than anything I'd ever expected of myself.

For some reason that thought brought tears to my eyes.

"That is really beautiful," Stephanie said and lightly touched my shoulder. "You are a true artist." She smiled at me before returning to collecting her things.

I *am* an artist, I thought. I really believed it. I could create something. It didn't have to be perfect, it just had to be honest —and part of me. That was what I thought this painting was.

"Lots of potential here, Samantha," the teacher said as she paused beside me. "I think you're going to do just fine in this class," she added. Then she walked to the front of the room.

"Attention, everyone, I have a surprise for all of you. On Thursday night, we're going to try something a little different. We're going to try living art," she said with a funny smile. "So don't be late!"

FIVE

When I got back to my apartment that night, my mind was still spinning a little. I was amazed at how much I'd learned from a bowl of fruit. But I also felt a little confused. For a long time I had felt as if I had an open mind, but one night at that class had shown me that I was still not seeing clearly.

I sat down with my computer and logged onto my blog. I decided to write about my realization, and how I felt as if my eyes were opening for the first time. I didn't think I would be seeing any of this if it weren't for the bucket list I'd been steadily checking off.

I had a few new comments from random readers of the blog, which I appreciated. But there was one comment in particular that I was waiting for.

When it appeared I felt an instant excitement. Blue was the first person to comment on my blog when I'd put it up. I had no idea who Blue was—male, female, young or old. But I felt a connection to Blue, strong enough that sometimes it seemed as if the posts I wrote were specifically written to this person.

What a journey you're on, SWF. I wish I was there to share it with you. I'm sure the moment that you actually got to "know" the fruit was exhilarating for you. I'm going to put together a bowl of fruit and spend a little time staring at it. Maybe I will learn to open my eyes as well.

I smiled as I read the words. It meant so much to me that, not only did someone find my blog interesting, but this particular commenter appeared to be joining me on my journey, as if every new discovery I made was something that this person could share in also. It felt as if I was inspiring someone, and having no idea who this person was made it even more thrilling.

I decided to comment back.

Don't forget the strawberries, Blue. They are big conversationalists.

I smiled and closed my computer.

Maybe I wasn't the best artist, but that was never my goal. I wanted to try new things, because I wanted to get to know who I was.

For many years I had defined myself by my job, by how I looked, by who my family was. I hadn't taken the time to actually know who *I* was. Now I had that opportunity and I was going to take it.

The next morning when I woke up for my shift at the Fluff and Stuff, I felt a sense of determination. I was going to see differently today. I was going to "know" the things I was looking at.

As I walked into the shop, I felt a new sense of life within me. I smelled the laundry detergent with new perspective. I touched the clothes I was folding with new appreciation.

When Old Joe walked in, I looked at him with new sight. He wasn't the crotchety old man that I usually saw him as. He had dimension, he had experience, he had stories written in the wrinkles of his skin.

"What the hell is wrong with you?" he snapped. "Are my socks clean or what?"

I blinked and reached for his basket of laundry waiting to be picked up.

"Here they are," I said smiling. "White as can be."

"Sure they are," he grumbled and handed me his payment.

He made his way out of the shop.

As the door swung shut behind him I stuck out my tongue. He might have dimension, but he was still grumpy. I didn't let his attitude ruffle my feathers. I was determined to have a good day.

I was hoping to see Max and talk about the class the night before, but he didn't stop by as I'd expected him to. Instead, the shop got busy, and by the time I was ready to close up, I realized Max wasn't coming at all.

It was unusual for me not to see him at least once a day.

I shook off the feeling of abandonment and focused on going through the motions of closing up. I wanted to get home and practice painting a banana.

As I was locking the door of the shop, I bumped into Stephanie, who was walking along the sidewalk.

"I'm glad I caught you!" she said with a big grin on her face.

I had given her a business card in case she wanted to have some laundry done.

"I can open back up," I said.

"Oh no, I was hoping you'd come out for a drink with me," Stephanie said, then frowned slightly. "I know that's a little odd—we don't know each other well—but, I've moved here recently and I don't have many friends in the area. So I thought maybe—" She sighed and shook her head. "This was probably a bad idea."

"It's not a bad idea at all," I said with a big smile.

I'd never had many female friends. I was friendly with my neighbor, who had helped me set up my blog, but when it came to actually hanging out and girl talk, I did most of that with Max. I thought this might be fun. "In fact there's a bar right around the corner we could go to if you would like," I said.

"Sounds great." Stephanie nodded.

As we walked, we chatted about the class the night before.

"I can't believe the teacher," I said. "She seems a little out there."

"Yes, she is. But she certainly can paint. I can't believe how quickly you caught on."

"She was right about seeing things in a different way," I went on as we entered the bar. "I never really thought of myself as being closed off, but today I'm seeing things with my eyes wide open."

"It's amazing, isn't it?" Stephanie asked.

As we shared a drink and spoke about our experiences in the class, I felt a strong connection with Stephanie. She seemed like someone I could definitely get along with.

"Drinking without me?" Max said accusingly as he settled onto a bar stool beside me.

"Max, hi!" I said, happy to see him. "This is my friend Stephanie."

He quirked a brow, probably shocked that I had a friend or shocked that I knew someone that he didn't—I wasn't sure which.

"Nice to meet you, Stephanie," he said with his flirty smile.

I narrowed my eyes.

He ignored me.

"You too, Max," she said. "Samantha and I were just discussing our painting class."

"Ah, the painting class." Max nodded. "I think it's great that Sammy is getting involved in something so creative."

"She's very talented," Stephanie said and smiled at me.

I looked from one to the other and could already see the sparks flying.

SIX

As the conversation continued, I stopped participating, because Max and Stephanie were talking about how much they had in common. It felt like I was just getting in the way.

"Excuse me, I'm going to use the restroom," I said as I stood up.

"Oh, I'll come with you." Stephanie jumped up and followed after me.

As we were washing our hands Stephanie looked at me in the mirror. "So, what's the story with you and Max?" she asked. "Are you together?"

I turned to look at her. I knew why she was asking. She was clearly interested in Max, and to my surprise, Max appeared to be genuinely interested in her. I wanted to lay claim to him, but I remembered my promise to myself. Max had gotten fourteen years, now it was time to move on.

"We've been best friends for years," I explained with a slow smile. "That's all we are—friends."

"So you wouldn't mind if we—"

"Not at all." I smiled so wide my jaw should have received hazard pay.

"Great!" she said with a sigh of relief. "He seems like a really great guy, but I didn't want to step on any toes."

"He is a really great guy," I said. "But he can be a bit of a player, so be careful," I added.

"Thanks for the warning." She laughed a little.

I didn't think she believed me.

As we walked back to the bar Max stood up to greet us.

"Another round?" he asked and turned to the bartender to order more drinks.

"Actually, I'm a little tired," I said with a shake of my head. "I think I'm going to head home. But you two should stay."

Max looked from me to Stephanie and then back to me.

"Are you sure?" he asked. "I could walk you—"

"I'm fine," I said. "Have fun." I spun on my heel and walked out of the bar.

Once outside I paused for a moment. I pretended it was to rummage through my purse for my keys. But I knew that wasn't why.

I was waiting for Max.

Waiting for him to choose me.

Again.

After a few minutes, I knew he wasn't coming.

I began walking back toward my apartment. I told myself I was doing the right thing.

When I got there I felt an ache in the pit of my stomach. I

knew that I'd had too many drinks—I knew I shouldn't, but I opened my computer.

I began typing away without thinking about what I was writing.

What is beautiful about being alone?

I clicked submit and was about to close the computer when it chimed, letting me know that I had a comment in response to my new blog post. Blue had already posted.

The beauty of being alone is the mystery of the people you have yet to meet.

I smiled at the words I read. I closed my computer and snuggled into bed with a warm glow within me. Maybe Blue was right. I needed to be less focused on what I lacked and more focused on the potential of what was to come.

The next night when I arrived at class, I was excited. I didn't even grill Stephanie to see how far the evening with Max had gone. I honestly didn't care.

Blue's words had sparked a sense of anticipation of what each moment would bring. I knew now that each person I met had the potential to be someone very influential in my life.

"Alright, class, settle down," the teacher said from the front of the room.

I noticed that she was dressed in her usual flowing gown, but her smile was a little nervous-looking tonight.

"Now, I have someone to introduce to you. We're all

adults here; I expect each of you to behave like it. Let's be mature and respectful and let's create some amazing art." She smiled proudly.

I raised an eyebrow. I was guessing that this was not about fruit.

"Sean!" she called out.

The door to the classroom opened and a man stepped into the room. He was drop-dead gorgeous with chiseled cheekbones and brooding brown eyes that seemed to see straight into my soul.

Okay, in truth he was a little handsome and well-built, but in my mind, he was a god.

"Oh boy," Stephanie said under her breath.

I glanced over at her. She wiggled her eyebrows at me. I wasn't sure what she was trying to communicate.

I watched as the man walked to the center of the room. I couldn't help but wonder why he would be wearing a bathrobe in the middle of a classroom, but then the teacher didn't exactly dress normally either, so I simply assumed that he was eccentric. I heard some whispering around me.

I glanced over at Stephanie but she was focused on the man at the front of the room.

I looked back in his direction and as I watched, he pushed the robe slowly back from his shoulders. It was halfway down his arms, exposing his solid chest.

My mouth dropped open slightly, as I was stunned. I took a breath and reminded myself to be mature about this. It was just his chest. It was nothing to be fussy about.

But then the robe dropped down to the floor around his feet, exposing his entire body.

I was fairly certain that the strangled squeaking sound I heard was coming from me.

Stephanie nudged my foot lightly with her own and I realized that I needed to close my mouth.

I looked away, and blushed, embarrassed by what I'd just seen.

SEVEN

Let's be honest, I'd seen naked men before, but it was just so unexpected.

I peeked back in his direction. He had placed his hands on his hips and settled into a comfortable stance. He was making no effort to cover himself up.

"I can see that a few of you are uncomfortable," the teacher said as she stood beside the naked man. "But I feel it's important that we paint the human body as it is designed. It is not designed to be covered in clothes. Would we dress up a banana?" she asked.

I had to tighten my lips to keep from giggling because she said banana and, well—she was standing next to his banana—it was all very hilarious in my opinion, but no one else was laughing so I did my best not to giggle.

"There should be no shame in nudity," the teacher continued. "Just as with the fruit we studied at our last class, in order to truly know another person, we must know their body, their skin, their texture." She nodded to the students.

"So let's see if we can create an image of this beautiful man with our paint and paintbrushes. Let's see if we can overcome our own shyness and celebrate what is only natural."

I was still thinking about bananas. Everyone else had begun painting. No one seemed to be as rattled as I was. I wanted to shout at all of them, "But he's naked!" but I didn't think that would go over well.

I stole a glance up at him again. He was staring casually into space. I was sure he had to be a professional model, because he seemed so comfortable just standing there. Even when I was alone in my apartment, I was rarely intentionally naked. Other than being in the shower and getting dressed, I always had something covering my body.

As I began to paint the features of the man before me, I recognized how strange that actually was. I was not comfortable walking around in just my skin, I had to have something hiding my body in order to feel normal.

I accentuated how relaxed his face was—how unconcerned he appeared to be. I doubted that I ever felt that comfortable, even when I was dressed. Although I noticed that Stephanie had no problem detailing things below the model's waist, I couldn't bring myself to even paint a belly button. Instead, I focused on his head, his face, his shoulders, the slope of his neck.

"Hmm," the teacher said. I jumped, as I hadn't even realized that she was beside me. "I like the detail," she said softly. "But I think you might want to explore other regions of his body."

I looked up at her shyly. "I guess I just find certain areas more interesting," I said.

"Or perhaps you feel a certain fear of a man's nakedness—of anyone's nakedness," the teacher suggested as she met my eyes. "It's nothing to be ashamed of. Many people are terrified of their own anatomy as well as the anatomy of others. But I can tell you this, once you learn to own your nudity—your completely nude body—it empowers you, and it also makes you more comfortable with the nudity of others."

I was beginning to feel like "nudity" was the word of the day and I had not studied. I was trying my hardest not to burst out into inappropriate laughter. Luckily she gave my shoulder a light pat and walked away. Of course I knew that what she was saying was absurd. I wasn't afraid of my naked body—or the naked body of anyone else.

"Alright, class, that's enough for tonight," she said. "Let's wrap it up."

I cupped my hand over my mouth and ducked my head. You're thirty-two, I kept reminding myself—do not laugh, do not laugh. I glanced over at Stephanie to find that she was hiding a smile too. But that only made things worse, because I really needed to burst out laughing.

Luckily, the model covered up and the bustle of the other students packing up their things distracted me from my laughter. By the time Stephanie and I stepped out of the classroom, though, we were both laughing.

"Do you think she even realized how funny that last remark was?" Stephanie asked with a giggle.

"I doubt it," I said in return and laughed loudly.

"I did think the model was amazing, though," Stephanie admitted. "Hopefully Max isn't the jealous type."

Those words made all my amusement fade away. "What do you mean?"

"I'm meeting him for coffee and a late-night snack."

"Oh." I tried to sound normal.

"You don't mind, do you?" she asked, looking concerned. "We really hit it off after you left the bar the other night. I can see why you've been friends for so long." She hesitated a moment and looked into my eyes. "Is there a reason why you two haven't been more than friends? Is that prying too much?"

I frowned and shook my head slowly. "It isn't prying," I said quietly. "I guess we just make better friends than anything else. Max has never been interested."

"Okay." She nodded. "Well, if it bothers you, just let me know. I like Max, but I've really enjoyed the two of us getting to be friends too."

"It won't bother me," I said.

But it did bother me. It bothered me more than I would ever admit to.

As she walked away I was glad that I wouldn't be seeing her again until the following Tuesday.

I was suddenly feeling determined not to see Max either.

EIGHT

I spent the weekend working on the painting I had started. From my memory, I tried to create the rest of the man's body. Every time I tried to paint anything below his hips I found my hand trembling. My eyes would water. I just couldn't imagine painting something so risqué.

Then I thought about what the teacher had said. Was I truly afraid of a man's body? Was I afraid of the bits and pieces that boxers traditionally covered? Weren't they as commonplace as a nose or an ear? What should be so different about them?

I recalled what the teacher had said about my own body. Was I scared of it?

Late Sunday night I stood in front of the mirror. I shed my clothes piece by piece until I was naked in front of the mirror. I had looked at myself without a shirt. I had looked at myself without pants, but I had very rarely taken a full gander at my entire nude body. I found it very difficult to look directly at my body. I could look at a part here and there, but to look at the entire image was a little daunting.

After a few moments, I forced myself to stare straight forward at the mirror. I was very used to looking in the mirror and finding something to criticize. Sometimes it was my weight, sometimes it was my skin, sometimes it was my posture, but it was always something I put myself down about. This time I stopped those thoughts and focused on the things I liked about my body.

It was even harder to think nice things about my body. That was a little surprising to me because I *was* confident. I liked to dress nicely, but I had never really said nice things about just my body.

I did the same thing on Monday night in preparation for returning to class the next night. I wanted to get familiar with my body, to be as comfortable in it as the man I had painted was. I also managed to add a few details to my painting. I was looking forward to sharing it with Stephanie and the teacher. I was proud of the progress that I'd made.

When I returned to class on Tuesday night, I was surprised to discover the teacher without her normally whimsical smile. She looked downright stressed out. She kept checking her watch and pacing back and forth.

"What's going on?" I whispered to Stephanie as I positioned my painting on my easel.

"Very nice," she said with a nod to my painting.

"Thank you." I smiled.

"Apparently the model that she had lined up for class tonight hasn't shown up," Stephanie said. "I heard her leaving a message for her a few minutes ago."

"Oh," I nodded.

I was a little disappointed. I was hoping it would be the same model we had painted the Thursday before. I had done the best I could from memory, but I was hoping to get another look to add a few finishing touches.

"I guess we'll have to cancel class tonight," the teacher said with a deep sigh. "Our model is not showing up, and I hadn't planned anything else for the evening."

I frowned and began packing up my paintbrushes. It was very disappointing. I had been looking forward to expanding my acceptance of the human body even more than I already had.

"Unless, of course, we have any volunteers?" the teacher called out.

I looked up with surprise.

"Did she say volunteers?" I asked Stephanie.

"I think so—" she began to say.

"Samantha, so kind of you to offer!" the teacher announced from the front of the room.

"Huh?" I looked up quickly to find that everyone in the room was staring at me. "I didn't volunteer." I shook my head quickly.

"You should do it," Stephanie encouraged me. "There's nothing more freeing than being naked in front of a crowd."

"Then maybe you should," I said with an edge to my voice.

"Oh no, I couldn't," Stephanie replied in a whisper. "I haven't groomed lately, if you know what I mean."

"Samantha, you really would make the perfect model," the teacher gushed as she walked toward me. "You have such a unique and voluptuous frame, I can only imagine how beautiful it would be on canvas."

All of the other students around me began clapping and nodding at the idea of me standing naked in front of them. I felt terrified and thrilled at the same time. I spent many years believing that no one would ever want to see me naked. Now I had an entire classroom full of people that wanted to see me nude.

Maybe that was the entire point of this experience. Not just to appreciate and express the beauty of others, but also to appreciate and express the beauty of my own body. The more I thought about it, the more I began to think it was what I had to do.

My brain screamed.

My body stood up anyway.

"What a wonderful gift you're offering us," the teacher said with a big smile. "Just get undressed."

Her words hit me like a polite but firm shove off a cliff.

Was I really going to do this?

I nervously began unbuttoning my shirt. The room was so quiet. I didn't think that anyone was even breathing.

A few of the students in the front of the class were politely averting their eyes, but the rest seemed to be fascinated by my fumbling fingertips. With each button I released I expected to turn and run out of the room. I didn't think I was actually going to be brave enough to follow through with what I was doing. Of all the things that I had done in my life —even those things that I had recently checked off my bucket list—this moment had to be the most horrifying. I knew that when my shirt fell back from my shoulders, I was going to be exposed to a room full of near-strangers.

"You're doing great, Samantha," my teacher said in a voice that reminded me of my seventh-grade music teacher.

NINE

I drew a deep breath and took my shirt off. I stood awkwardly with it in my hand for a moment. It seemed rude to just drop it on the floor. There are rules. Even in public nudity

I started folding it up as neatly as I could.

"Here, I'll take that," the teacher said with a smile.

Then my shirt was gone. It wasn't on the floor beside me where I could grab it if I needed it.

She whisked it away and I had no idea where she put it.

Another deep breath and my jeans were unbuttoned. I closed my eyes and pushed them down over my hips. Then over my knees. Then over my ankles.

"I'll take those too," the teacher said.

My shirt was gone. My jeans were gone. I was standing in front of the class in nothing but a bra and panties. I refused to open my eyes.

"Now everyone notice the way her skin tone is nearly flawless," the teacher instructed.

I felt a hint of pride at her words, but also a new wave of terror.

"Please continue, Samantha," she said in a softer voice.

"I think this is enough," I blurted out. "I mean, there's plenty of curves to paint."

"Samantha, it's a nude study," the teacher said. "If you're not comfortable, we can see if someone else might like to volunteer."

I could feel myself blushing. I was already mostly nude. If I quit now, all of my embarrassment would be for nothing. It was just one night. Just one class. But it was a huge step for me, I knew that. If I really wanted to know who I was and what I was made of, it was time to take the biggest risk I could muster.

I closed my eyes and shed the remainder of my clothing. Slowly I opened my eyes again. I could see all of the students in the class in front of me. No one seemed to be complaining.

After a few minutes of no one throwing tomatoes or demanding that I cover up, I began to relax a little. It was so normal to wear clothing. It was what was expected of me—of anyone walking down the street—to cover their body. Yet being without clothes was exactly the way the teacher had described it—extremely liberating.

I couldn't be sure if I was happy or if I had just gone numb, but I began to settle into my own skin. I felt as if the world was so different when I didn't have to think about the clothes that I was wearing or hiding certain parts of myself. I was out in the open for all to see, and despite the horror I had experienced a few minutes before, now I felt absolutely no shame.

The pencils and paintbrushes were skimming across the papers. The teacher was gently gasping as she walked between the easels, murmuring words of support. All of this was happening because I had been brave enough to walk up to the front of the room and shed all of my clothes—every last stitch.

My stomach fluctuated from that feeling of excited butterflies to sinking with fear at being so exposed. It was a thrilling experience and one I realized I would never have again. A person only had their first naked parade in front of strangers once in their lifetime, and this was my special day.

When the teacher lightly clapped her hands to get the attention of the students, she drew me out of my wandering thoughts. "Alright, everyone, we need to finish up for tonight. You've all done a wonderful job. Let's show Samantha just how much we appreciate her willingness to volunteer," she added.

The entire class began applauding me. There was something distinctly delectable about being applauded while naked. I felt as if I should bow, but to my credit, I resisted.

"Samantha?" the teacher said again to get my attention.

I looked over at her to find that she was handing me my clothes.

"Oh, thank you." I took my clothes and turned back to the class.

Everyone was packing up their supplies. I was no longer the focus of attention.

I dressed awkwardly, as if each piece of clothing I put on reminded me of my own nakedness. Maybe if I had stayed nude, I never would have remembered at all.

"Thanks again, Samantha," the teacher said once I was dressed. She gave me a light pat on the shoulder.

"Of course." I smiled. "It's all just between us, anyway. It was actually a very enlightening experience. And it's not like any of these paintings are going to see the light of day."

"Not so much the light of day—just the lights at the art show," the teacher said with a laugh as she began straightening the items on her desk.

"What?" I said as the words "art" and "show" spun through my mind so fast that I thought I might pass out.

"Yes, didn't I mention it?" the teacher asked.

I was beginning to think this flighty behavior was all an act. No one could truly be so ditzy.

"No, you didn't mention it," I said through gritted teeth.

"All of the live studies will be entered into the local art show—it's part of the class project," the teacher explained. "It gives all of these budding artists the chance to have a real gallery experience."

"A real gallery experience with my naked body?"

As in strangers? With eyeballs?

"Don't I have to sign some kind of release for that?"

"Well, actually, you did sign it when you signed up for the class," the teacher said. "And since you volunteered to model, consent is implied."

"No, no—it is *not* implied." I was feeling more than a little freaked out.

All of the other students had already emptied out of the classroom. The teacher actually looked a little frightened of me.

"I'm sorry for the confusion, but if we don't have something to enter, all of the students will be left out of the show," she said with a frown. "You wouldn't want to ruin that for them, would you? Besides, you have nothing to be ashamed of. The paintings came out beautifully."

The paintings. My heart flipped. I wondered how people had depicted me. I knew that I never photographed well, so the paintings had to be pretty terrible. I was starting to panic.

"This was a huge mistake," I said, frowning.

"Aw." The teacher gently squeezed my shoulder. "Samantha, it was no mistake. One day you'll see that," she assured me. "I have to get going now," she added. "We're the last ones to leave."

Still in shock, I followed her out of the room.

I watched her lock the door. Then we continued out of the school.

By the time I reached the parking lot, I realized the teacher was gone.

I turned back to look at the school and was still stunned to think that there was a room full of naked paintings of me inside.

TEN

That night, I could not get to sleep. I kept thinking about the paintings. I didn't want anyone to see them. I couldn't believe what I had done. I had let myself get caught up in the ideals of an art teacher. She wasn't the one that had gotten naked, now was she?

Finally I climbed out of bed. I knew what had to be done.

I dressed quickly and stepped out of my apartment. I found Max walking up to my door.

"Can we talk?" he asked as I started to brush past him.

"I have somewhere to be," I said.

"This late?" he asked, looking surprised.

"Please, Max, not now," I said quickly. I didn't have time to discuss why I had been avoiding him.

"Alright," Max said with confusion in his voice.

For once, I didn't obsess about what he was thinking. I needed to get to the paintings and fast.

When I arrived at the school, I had no real plan, except that I had to get inside. The school was still dark. I could see that there were a few exit signs glowing in the front hallway. For a split second I wondered if there was an alarm system.

The truth was, it didn't matter. If I was going down, I was going down clothed.

I tried the front door, hoping that by some stroke of luck I would be able to simply walk in. It was locked. I sighed and walked the length of the building. I noticed that there was a window open near a back door. It wasn't open much. Maybe one of the high school teachers had cracked it during the day for a quick smoke and forgotten to close it.

But it was open enough. I pushed it up the rest of the way and climbed inside.

I hurried out of the classroom and down the hall to the art room that was reserved for our classes. I flipped on the light and was greeted by me—naked and all over the room. I stared at the paintings spread out before me.

I had broken into the classroom so that I could destroy all of the paintings, but now that I was looking at them, I felt a slow, unexpected swell of awe.

They hadn't painted flaws.

They'd painted strength.

They weren't the ugly paintings I had expected them to be. Each person had painted my unadorned body with their own special perspective. Each one had accentuated a different aspect of my body, so that even I couldn't find a way to deny the beauty on the canvas. I was so enthralled by the sight that I didn't hear the quiet sound of the door behind me sliding open.

"Wow," Max said from behind me.

I jumped and bumped into the easel in front of me.

"Max!" I gasped and tried to shield the painting from view.

There was no point, as there were more than a dozen nearly identical paintings spread out across the room for him to see. "Close your eyes!" I said. "Close your eyes this instant!"

"Are these you, Sammy?" he asked with shock and delight in his voice. "Is this how you've been spending your evenings?"

"Max!" I nearly shouted. "Please, don't look." My voice trembled. He looked over at me and met my eyes.

"Don't be upset," he said softly. "They're beautiful."

For a moment, I saw myself the way he did.

And that was far more terrifying than the nudity.

"Max, they're not for you to see."

"Is that why you broke in here?" he asked. "I followed you because I knew that you were up to something."

"I was going to destroy them," I said with a frown. "I didn't want anyone else seeing them."

"Well, that would be a shame," he said with a slight shake of his head. "One day you'll have to accept your beauty, Sammy, whether you like it or not."

I stared back at him with disbelief.

In the distance I could hear sirens. Had someone reported the break-in or was I just being paranoid?

"Let me take you home," Max said. "Leave the paintings."

"I can get there myself," I said quietly.

"Sam, are we okay?" he asked with concern in his eyes.

"We will be. But I can get home by myself. And I can

decide to get into trouble on my own—without you needing to get me out of it. I don't need you to take care of me, Max."

"I know you don't," he said softly.

"Good," I said and pushed past him.

If he followed me I didn't know it; I didn't look back.

When I arrived back at my apartment, I sat down with my computer. I tapped out another blog post, detailing how startling it was to see my body through the eyes of others and how refreshing it could be to finally be able to see yourself from another perspective.

I waited a few minutes to see if Blue would post.

Then I shut off my computer and went to bed. Soon more people than had ever seen me naked would be seeing my body, as it was interpreted by a variety of budding artists.

Surprisingly, I was okay with that.

For once, I wasn't hiding.

#5 RUN A MARATHON

ONE

When my alarm went off, I was violently expelled from an amazing dream. I was on a sailboat, journeying across a vast ocean. I was alone, but I wasn't afraid. I was perfectly confident that I was capable of making it to my destination. I felt vital and enlivened by the freedom that rushed through me with every rolling wave.

When I opened my eyes to the reality of my life, I found myself instantly crushed by the routine of it. In an hour I would need to be at Fluff and Stuff to open it up for the day. Then I would have some coffee, read the paper, and obsess about the state of the world, country, or city depending on what article I read.

Once a customer arrived to distract me, I would lose myself in the routine of my work. I might be interrupted by Max showing up for a chat. I might flip on the old television and watch a soap opera just to spice up my day.

But in the end, I would close up the shop and head back to my small apartment, alone, and with nothing more important to do than turn on the television so that I wouldn't miss one of my several favorite shows.

Lately, my life had been more adventurous. But apparently, I had a talent for re-rutting.

I wanted to be interesting—to be valid and worthy. I wanted to matter in some way. I wanted a reason to wake up before my alarm went off, with an eagerness to participate in my life rather than a sense of obligation.

I climbed out of bed and headed for the shower.

As I walked across the room, I grumbled at the tension in my back, the soreness of my knees, and the general unpleasantness of waking up to a stiff body. I sighed as I walked past the tall mirror that hung from the back of my closet door. I had lost quite a bit of weight recently and my body certainly looked better, but it hadn't changed much in the past few weeks. I had hit a plateau despite sticking fairly well to my diet.

I knew that the main problem was lack of movement. I had been so caught up lately in my routine that I had forgotten to get out and exercise. I needed something more than just heading to the gym. I could do that any old time. It was boring.

I wanted a challenge—something that would make me feel a little more competitive and a little less bored.

As I walked the few blocks to Fluff and Stuff, I noticed a few familiar faces. Since I walked on nearly the same schedule each day, I'd become acquainted with certain sights.

There was the blue-haired lady who walked her Pomeranian. There was the hot dog vendor who didn't seem to comprehend that people did not want to eat hot dogs for breakfast.

Then there were the runners. They were always moving too fast for me to name them in particular, so I just named the group of them—the runners.

They were always decked out in bright green or yellow running gear. Most of the time, I avoided looking at them, but today, for some reason, I couldn't look away.

Today it struck me that *that* was what I wanted. I wanted to wake up each morning and go after life, not at a casual walk, but at a run.

I was sure that I could do it. It would take some time for me to build up my speed, but I had the time to do that.

I was so inspired that I sped up to a jog for the rest of the way to work.

I'd worked up a bit of a sweat by the time I arrived at the laundromat. I unlocked the door and prepared for the day by checking all of the washers and dryers and making sure that the items in the small shop were all in the right places.

But my mind was on the runners.

The ache of my feet told me one particular thing, however. If I was going to become a runner, I would need better shoes.

The thought reminded me of something on my bucket list.

One of the items I wanted to accomplish, now that I was in better shape physically, was to run a marathon. It had seemed out of reach in the past. After my short jog along the block it *still* seemed very much out of reach. But it was on the list, and I was feeling just brave enough to check it off. Of course it would probably take several months of training to be ready, but before that, it would take one of my favorite things —shopping!

I spent my free time at work researching running shoes on my phone. If I was going to do this, I had to do it right, of course.

As soon as another employee showed up to cover the evening shift, I headed out to browse the shoe store a few blocks away. I was determined that whatever I bought would not end up in my "closet of no return."

The "closet of no return" was a closet off of my kitchen. Inside this closet, were the ghosts of exercise fads past. I had everything from balance balls to ab zappers in there. All things I was sure I would use every day—that had been relegated to the closet within a week. It had taken me a long time —and several hundred dollars—to realize there was no quick fix. Apparently, sweat was non-refundable.

TWO

When I stepped into the shoe store, the scent of leather greeted me in a way that made me feel excited and a little frightened. This wasn't a heel and pump store, this was a real sports store. There were images of athletes plastered all over the walls. Of course my body didn't look anything like those on the posters, but I did my best to ignore that.

As I walked down the aisles, I reminded myself that I was on a journey and this was just one step of it.

I stood in front of the rows and rows of running shoes. I had no idea which ones I should buy. I was someone who spent a fair amount of money on shoes to go with my dresses and fancier outfits, but I had rarely put much thought into what kind of sneakers to wear. Nor did I have any idea how many there were; and the variety of colors was mind-boggling. There was even a pair that I was sure would make my feet look like rainbows if I were to wear them.

As I picked up a pair and studied them, I noticed

someone a few rows down. It was Stephanie, a woman I had met in the art class that I'd been taking recently.

"Hey, Stephanie." I smiled as I walked up to her.

"Samantha, it's so good to see you. I was wondering why you didn't come back to art class?"

"Uh, well—" I blushed a little. "—I figured that everyone had seen enough of me."

"I guess so." Stephanie laughed a little at the inside joke.

"Are you shopping for running shoes too?" I asked.

"Yes, I was thinking about signing up for the Mountain Marathon."

"Me too," I said, surprising myself. "I mean, it would be my first one, but I thought it might be fun to try something new—get out there in the community a little."

"It will be," Stephanie assured me. "I ran in something similar last year, and the enthusiasm of the people is just incredible. I can't wait to experience it again." She paused a moment and looked thoughtful. "We should train together," she added. "Would you like to? We could get together each morning until the race—I mean if you want to."

"That would be great," I said, a little surprised that she was so willing.

I was still getting used to having a female friend. I hadn't been sure if she would still want to hang out after the last art class we'd shared. Not to mention that I was fairly certain she and Max were still seeing each other. I felt a little queasy at that thought. I was used to seeing the women Max was with as vapid and ditzy, and I didn't see Stephanie that way.

"Great, let's meet tomorrow morning—around six?" she

said. "We can run down by the pond off of Third. Do you know it?"

"I've seen it." I nodded.

I was a little thrown by two things about her invitation. Actually, I was more thrown by the idea of arriving somewhere by six in the morning, as well as the word "run." I wasn't even sure if I could sustain a swift jog, let alone run. I didn't want to miss out on the chance to spend more time with Stephanie, though—and it was on my list, after all.

"I can do that." I cringed. "But I should warn you, I'm a little out of shape."

"Don't worry," she said quickly. "We'll take it at your pace. No one starts out as a runner, Samantha," she assured me. "Make sure you get some shoes with good ankle support. Wear them as much as you can so you can break them in."

"Alright. I will."

"I'll see you tomorrow," Stephanie called out as she headed to the register.

I nodded and waved.

I was sure that I should have told her "maybe" so that I'd have an excuse for not showing up that early, but I was hoping that the commitment would make me force myself to be there. Change didn't happen simply because I wanted it to. Change happened because I actively made it happen.

With this in mind, I grabbed a pair of very bright green shoes and slipped them on my feet. They were a perfect fit. With these emerald shoes on, I felt as if I could run around the globe—I could run down highways and through tunnels.

I caught sight of them in one of those ankle-high mirrors and started to step forward to get a closer look. What I hadn't planned on was the tiny clear piece of plastic that tied the two shoes together.

I stumbled and windmilled my arms like a malfunctioning scarecrow. Unfortunately, the only thing around me to grab was a tower of shoeboxes. I knew that it was a bad idea, but in the split second before falling to the ground, there wasn't a lot of time to think it through.

I grabbed hold of the tower of shoeboxes as I fell forward. Of course the tower simply gave way as a result of my futile grasping, and the entire pile of shoeboxes fell directly on top of me after I had landed hard on the carpeted floor of the shop.

From beneath the pile of boxes, I could hear the sounds of people gasping and muttering. I heard the distinct footsteps of someone in charge approaching me.

I could only hope that Stephanie had made it out of the store before I had embarrassed myself so thoroughly.

THREE

I hadn't even thought about how I actually felt and whether I might have injured myself. Of course the thought that I might have twisted my ankle sparked some hope that I wouldn't have to arrive anywhere at six in the morning.

"Ma'am," a deep voice asked from beyond the pile of shoeboxes. "Are you hurt?"

I didn't want to answer. I didn't want to think about what had just happened, or how many people would be staring at me when I emerged from my cavern of shoeboxes.

"I'm fine. I just need a minute."

"Ma'am, let me help you," the voice said. Its owner picked up one of the shoeboxes blocking my face. I looked up into deep green eyes, curly blond hair, and about twenty years of life. I couldn't help but notice that his pink lips were struggling to hide a grin.

Reluctantly I sat up, knocking more boxes off my back. I did my best not to look at the stares around me.

"Sorry about the mess," I said quietly. "But they really

should put a warning on these things, you know. I mean, why would they use clear plastic to tie shoes together? Who is going to see that?"

"Well—uh—most people," the manager said as he collected a few more shoeboxes from around me. "Are you planning on buying those?"

"I suppose I am."

Luckily, most of the other customers had returned to their shopping.

I was mortified, but it was something I was becoming accustomed to. It seemed to me that if it could happen to anyone, it usually happened to me.

"Here, let me get that." He pulled a small pair of scissors from his pocket. He reached down and cut the plastic that held the two shoes together. "There you go," he said as if he was talking to a child. "All better now."

I stared at him for a long moment. It was hard to imagine that I was ever his age—young and arrogant, believing that the world was designed just for me. It was hard for me to imagine still having that bright shimmering in my eyes indicating that the best was yet to come.

"Thank you. Do you want me to help you with this?" I gestured to the mess of boxes.

"No, that's alright. Trust me—it happens all the time."

"Really?"

"Well, not exactly like this." He laughed a little. "Usually it's kids that knock them over, but it's just a pile of shoes. You know—no big deal."

I smiled at him. Maybe I needed a little more of that

shiny young optimism. It really was just a pile of shoes—no big deal.

I took off the shoes and slipped my old ones back on. I followed the manager up to the register and paid for them, doing my best to avoid eye contact.

When I stepped out of the store, I tried to leave the embarrassing moment behind me. I had a marathon to run, and I couldn't let anything stop me.

I returned to my apartment and took a long warm bath. Then I headed to bed early, so I would be bright and cheerful when my alarm went off at five-thirty.

When the blaring, mind-jarring sound of my alarm went off the next morning, the alarm clock somehow went sailing across the room. Luckily, it landed on a discarded pillow on the floor and bounced safely to the carpet. It continued to blare obnoxiously.

I groaned and forced myself to sit up in bed. I was not much of a morning person and certainly not when I was expecting to exercise for the first time in months.

Still, I didn't want to disappoint Stephanie, and now there was no way to get to my alarm clock without getting out of bed.

I rolled over until I was half out of the bed and half in it. I stretched out my foot and tried to hit the snooze button with the tip of my toe. I only managed to push it further out of my reach. I stretched out my foot a little farther, determined to shut the alarm off. Unfortunately, that caused the rest of my body to slide off the edge of my mattress, and I tumbled onto the floor. I landed with my head inches from the alarm, which continued screaming like it had won.

"Enough!" I shouted and smacked the alarm clock until it was finally quiet.

I lay there for a few minutes, debating whether to get up.

Eventually, I pushed myself up off the floor. I stumbled around blearily until I had clothes on and my brand new running shoes tied tight. Then I grabbed my purse and keys and headed out of the apartment.

Morning looked a lot different at quarter 'til six. People were rushing to their cars, school buses were rumbling by, the trash truck was ridiculously loud.

I wondered how I had slept through so much noise all these years.

I started my car and thought about turning it back off. I could always say I overslept or that I ate something funny—or just not call Stephanie at all. I closed my eyes for a moment and tried to remember why I had even put "running a marathon" on my bucket list.

I remembered watching a marathon when I was about sixteen. I remembered seeing the passion in the faces of the runners as they ran, knowing they had a long way to go, but still valuing each step.

I had taken a life lesson from that at the time—that a journey may be long, a destination may be far—but each step matters.

FOUR

This was one of my steps.

I had no idea what the destination was. I had no idea how long the journey would be, but this was a step on it and one that mattered. I had spent too much time being afraid to move forward in life, letting steps pass me by.

My bucket list was not just about doing fun things that I'd always hoped to do. It was about seizing opportunities in life that I had almost allowed to pass me by. So, this was the next step in my journey. I was not going to take that step by crawling back into bed and hiding from something that was challenging. I was going to take it, by shifting my car into gear and driving to that pond where Stephanie would be meeting me.

It was time to leave behind the idea of fear and believe in my own bravery. That was the type of person I knew myself to be—strong, determined, and adventurous.

Soon I found myself parking in the parking lot beside the

pond. I barely remembered the drive there, but I was feeling a little more inspired.

The air was crisp and cool as I drew it deep into my lungs. I felt how invigorating it could be to really breathe.

A quick glance around showed me that Stephanie had not arrived yet.

I walked over to a bench near the path and decided to look the part rather than just standing there. I pulled one foot up behind me and stretched my leg as I leaned forward. It felt good to truly expand my body. I switched to my other leg and nearly lost my balance. Luckily, the bench was there for me to grab onto and steady myself.

Back on two feet, I glanced around the path. It was a paved path that wrapped around a mid-sized pond. It was frequented by daily joggers, dog walkers, and moms pushing strollers. I had driven by it many times, but had never really taken the time to stop and explore the place.

A little nature was very refreshing. Of course the hustle and bustle of the city was not far off.

"Samantha!" Stephanie called out from the parking lot. "Sorry I'm late," she continued as she jogged over to me.

She had her dark hair tied back in a ponytail and was wearing an adorable set of plum-shaded workout clothes. I, of course, was in sweat pants, a ratty old t-shirt, and my brand new sneakers, which I now felt were far too green.

"It's okay. I was just doing a little stretching," I said and smiled nervously at her. I enjoyed hanging out with her, but I was still waiting for her to tire of me.

"Good idea," she said and stretched her arms high above

her head. "I got caught up with Max this morning," she added.

Max and this morning screamed in my head. Did that mean she went to a super early breakfast with him or did that mean that he'd spent the night?

I knew what it meant, to be honest. Max had no problem finding his way into bed with women. He was charming, with a decent build and a romantic nature when it suited him. But it still made me uneasy to think about it.

Focus, I snapped at myself. You're here to train for a marathon, not to think about Max.

"Let's warm up," Stephanie said. "We can just do a quick lap around the pond and then we'll figure out how many we feel up to."

I stared at her for a moment. "Around the whole pond?" I asked.

"Yes," she said, laughing. "You're so funny, Samantha."

I wasn't joking. That path was pretty long. She thought that was a warm-up? Brave, I reminded myself—brave and adventurous. I took a deep breath and nodded.

"Let's do it!"

"Great!" Stephanie cheered. She began running toward the path.

I loped after her.

Everything about Stephanie was bouncy. She bounced from foot to foot as she jogged. Her long thick hair was bouncy. Her perfectly formed breasts were quite bouncy.

Behind her, I felt like a potato that had sprouted legs for the first time. I wobbled, my pace irregular and throwing me off balance.

I tried to keep up with Stephanie, but the faster I jogged the tighter my chest felt. Not to mention the fact that I kept coming down at an awkward angle on my ankle, and a twinge of pain was shooting up my calf with each stride.

Stephanie kept getting further and further away from me.

At some point she wasn't even Stephanie, my new friend, anymore. She was every woman that I felt I couldn't measure up to or keep up with.

I knew that was unreasonable. Stephanie had never been anything but nice to me. But she had the figure I wanted, she had the confidence I craved, she had the man I had been crushing on for over ten years.

How could I not feel some jealousy building within me? But that jealousy also sparked a fire within me and a determination to catch up with her.

I pushed myself harder and ignored the burning of my lungs and the screaming of my knees.

I was almost a foot away from her when I tripped over absolutely nothing. I mean, there was nothing on the path, nothing darted out in front of me, nothing caught my toe.

I just fell, because I was me—because my face needed to be introduced to the path.

FIVE

Stephanie must have heard the thump and my groan. She stopped and turned to face me. "Oh my gosh, Samantha, are you okay?" She knelt down in front of me. "Are you hurt?"

"I'm okay," I muttered in reply and pushed myself up off the ground. "Just a little bump in the road."

Stephanie swept her eyes over the path. "Usually they keep it pretty clear," she said. "Are you sure that you're okay?"

"I'm fine." I nodded. "I guess I just couldn't keep up," I admitted with a sigh.

"Why didn't you just tell me to slow down?" Stephanie said. "I didn't realize how much trouble you were having."

"I thought I could keep up."

"Samantha, this is your first marathon. It's going to take time for you to find your rhythm." She smiled.

"My rhythm?" I asked as I leaned against one of the benches close to the water.

"Yes, your body will tell you what pace is right for you. If you find that you're having a hard time maintaining a certain speed, slow it down a notch or two. If you go full force every time you run, you'll never find your natural rhythm. A marathon isn't about sprinting, it's about maintaining. If you want to make it to the end, you have to find your steady pace."

"I see," I nodded, still feeling a little embarrassed. "I just wanted to do well."

"And you are," Stephanie said with an encouraging smile. "Why don't we try a swift walk, and we can figure out what works best for you?"

"You don't mind? I don't want to hold you back."

"Nonsense, I'm looking forward to getting a chance to talk with you."

We fell into step together. It was nice not to feel my lungs burning.

"I love being out at this time of day," Stephanie said. "It's like the day is new."

I smiled at her words. I had to agree with her. There was something calming about knowing that I still had the whole day ahead of me.

"So, how have things been going with you and Max?" I asked.

I cringed. Why, why, why, did I ask that? It had just popped out of my mouth, unplanned. Now I would have to hear the answer.

"Oh, you know—we're keeping things casual," Stephanie said with a distant smile. "Seems to be the way he prefers it."

I bit my tongue to keep from telling her that what he actually preferred was a different girl every week. I was in a tough place. I knew that Max was a bit of a player and I wanted Stephanie to become a good friend. But I couldn't betray Max either.

"Well, I'm glad you hit it off," I said, and immediately regretted it.

"Me too." Stephanie shrugged. "I swear, it's so funny. All I hear about is Sammy this and Sammy that. I feel like I already know you pretty well."

I was stunned by her words. "He talks about me?" I asked, surprised.

"All the time." Stephanie nodded. "He told me about the vacation you two went on together. He said it was the most fun he'd ever had on a trip."

"It was fun." I nodded. "Max and I always have fun." I cringed as I heard my own words. "I mean—as friends."

"Friends—of course." Stephanie glanced over at me.

I could tell that she wanted to ask me something more, but I avoided looking back at her. I hoped she would drop the subject.

"He seems so dedicated to his work," she continued. "That's nice to see."

"I guess. I've never understood what he finds so fascinating about computers." I laughed a little.

"Well, if it makes him happy," Stephanie said with a smile. "I love to see people passionate about what they do. It makes them more passionate about other areas in their lives—if you know what I mean." She wiggled her eyebrows.

I thought I might vomit. Maybe it was the exercise catching up with me, but I was pretty sure it was the idea of Max being "passionate" with Stephanie.

"You know what?" I gasped out as I slowed my pace. "I think I've had enough for today."

"Oh, really?" Stephanie said with a frown. "Are you sure?"

"I'll do better tomorrow," I said, taking another deep breath.

"Good, because you know the race is on Sunday."

"Sunday?" I laughed. "Very funny."

"I'm serious." Stephanie frowned. "Didn't you see the updated flier?"

"Huh?" I stared at her with disbelief, still hoping that she was joking.

"Yes. They moved the race up a month because of the bad weather last year. They're hoping to avoid any rain," she said.

"There's no way I'll be ready by then."

"You'll do fine," Stephanie assured me. "Just meet me here tomorrow. We'll get your body nice and loosened up, and you can do the best you can at the marathon."

"I could probably show up," I said, nodding my head but feeling more skeptical about the whole idea.

"I think you might surprise yourself, Samantha," Stephanie said with confidence.

It was nice to have someone believe in me, but it also made me question Stephanie's sanity.

"Alright, I'll meet you tomorrow."

"Great!" Stephanie grinned. "I'll bring us smoothies!"

"Great," I replied and managed a smile before I limped off to my car.

SIX

I proceeded to spend the rest of my day flipping out.

I had no idea what I had gotten myself into. My legs were sore, I was tired from waking up way too early, and the marathon was on Sunday!

There was nothing I could do to stop this from happening. I had already told Stephanie that I would do it, and she would likely tell Max. I couldn't have Max believing that I was too lazy to do what I said I would do. I had been absolutely out of my mind to think I could do this in the first place.

By the time I returned to my apartment that night, I'd decided that I would have to claim some terrible disease that would magically be cured by Monday.

I had spent some of my shift at work looking up short-lived, easily faked, highly contagious diseases. I was debating between shingles—dramatic but questionable—or influenza—classic, dependable, socially acceptable—when my phone rang and the rash photo disappeared.

It was Max.

"Hello?" I asked, hesitating slightly.

"Hey there," he said with that familiar, easy tone that made my insides melt. "I hear you've been busy."

"Maybe," I said and then coughed. "I haven't been feeling too well."

Then I frowned. Did people with shingles cough? I had a feeling I was stuck with influenza.

"Oh, that's too bad," Max said. "I was hoping maybe I could come by some time. We haven't had a lot of Max and Sammy time."

"That's true," I said, my heart pounding.

Even with Stephanie to occupy him, he was still thinking of me. That was a good sign, wasn't it? I shifted uncomfortably. Was I hoping that he wanted to be with me more? I felt a little guilty for it.

"But if you're not feeling well..." he said quickly. "I'm sure that you need your rest."

"No, no, I'm better," I said and immediately felt foolish. "You should come over tomorrow. I work the morning shift, so I should be home by the time you get off work. I mean—unless you have other plans," I added.

"Other plans?" he asked with shock in his voice. "No other plans could ever stop me from seeing you, Sam," he said, being his normal charming self.

I tried to ignore the quickening of my heartbeat. I was supposed to be getting over Max, not getting jealous over him.

"Alright, I'll see you tomorrow then," I said.

"I'll be there," he said and clicked off the phone.

The picture of the rash popped back up on the screen. I grimaced and deleted it. There was no way I was going to get out of this. I remembered what the young man at the shoe store had said to me. "It's not a big deal."

Like Stephanie had said, I would run in the marathon and that would be that.

I decided I needed a little more motivation. My blog was the perfect place to get that. Once I put down in words what I was experiencing, I knew that I wouldn't be able to take it back.

I opened my computer and began tapping on the keyboard. I had to admit that even my fingertips hurt a little bit. I was determined to get my feelings out about running.

As I described the sensation of liberation—to run like I had once as a child—I found myself smiling at the memory of it. Of course I admitted to face-planting. I also detailed what it was like to feel as if I had to earn my place running beside Stephanie.

I described finding my own pace.

I didn't know for sure that my words would help anyone, but I imagined I wasn't the only person in the world who felt the way I did. I knew there would be at least one pair of eyes reading my words.

Blue. I had come to look forward to reading any comment that Blue left. I knew it was a little silly of me to feel as if I had some kind of bond with a complete stranger on the Internet. I didn't even know if Blue was male or female, old or some young teen, but it didn't matter. Blue always appreciated what I had to say and even offered advice at times.

When I submitted the blog post, I felt like I had just

spoken to a priest. Everything was out in the open and off my chest. I felt lighter.

I waited for a few minutes. I pretended that I was not waiting for a sign that Blue had left a comment.

I checked my e-mail. I surfed some news sites.

But the truth was, I *was* waiting. I was hoping.

When I heard no chime telling me that there was a new comment, I finally closed my computer.

I crawled into bed, my sore body eager to collapse.

When my alarm went off in the morning, I was determined not to throw it. I knew that would only result in my likely having to buy another alarm clock.

Anyway, the blog post I'd written the night before was on my mind. I wanted to see if Blue had left a comment yet. So I pulled myself out of bed and headed for my computer.

I opened it up and logged into my blog. I scanned quickly and immediately saw a post from Blue. I smiled at the sight of it.

A new adventure for you. I'm sure that you will accomplish it. Please post a picture of you crossing the finish line.

Those words made my excitement fade a little.

A picture? I wasn't sure if I was willing to do that. My anonymous blog would become much more personal if I did.

But I also felt a little thrilled that Blue wanted to witness my victory. It felt like a true friendship to me.

My heart beat a little faster as I got ready to meet Stephanie. I was ready to seize the day, knowing that Blue was expecting that picture. I wasn't going to be able to flake out now. I would have to have something to post.

SEVEN

My run with Stephanie was uneventful. There wasn't much chatting between us. I was pushing myself harder than ever. I wanted to be able to make it to the finish line, and that meant that I had to train a little harder.

In my mind, it was Blue waiting for me at the finish line. Whoever Blue was, they were someone who believed in me, and that was enough motivation for me to keep moving.

Stephanie was still pacing herself slower than normal—I could tell—but she was complimenting me on the progress I had made. I just kept my head down and kept moving. No more distractions.

No more thinking about Max and Stephanie together. No more worrying what I looked like in my workout gear or how bright my green shoes were.

This was about a mission, and I was going to get through it.

However, by the time I drove to Fluff and Stuff, my legs were screaming. I had certainly made them angry.

I spent most of my day at work sitting down. I sat to fold clothes, I sat to sort clothes. I hobbled to switch clothes from the washer to the dryer. By the time my relief showed up, I was desperate for my bed.

It wasn't until I arrived at my apartment that I remembered I was supposed to be meeting Max. The way my body felt, all I wanted was to escape, to evade the possibility of being seen in my debilitated state.

I had my phone out to text Max so that I could cancel our get-together, but before I could send it, there was a knock on the door. I knew that it had to be Max.

"Come in," I called out, knowing that he would never just turn around and leave now. I continued to limp my way into the kitchen. "I'm in the kitchen," I called out when I heard the door open and close.

"What are you up to?" Max said from the living room.

I grabbed two bags of frozen vegetables from the freezer. Then I waddled back to the living room. I sank down into the easy chair beside the sofa and dropped a bag on each knee.

"Ugh," I sighed.

"Here I thought you were going to make me dinner." Max laughed as he sat down on the sofa. "What have you done to yourself?"

"What have I done?" I repeated in a contemplative tone. "I have been training for a marathon."

"A marathon?" he repeated. "Is that what you and Stephanie have been up to?"

"She told you?" I asked, surprised.

"Well, she mentioned that she was running with you," he said with some hesitation in his voice.

I could tell that he was feeling a little awkward.

"Stephanie is a great person," I said and narrowed my eyes at him. "You better be nice to her."

"I'm always nice," Max shot back with some hurt in his voice. He was silent for a moment and then slid forward to the edge of the sofa. "So what do you two talk about when you run?"

I raised an eyebrow and met his eyes intently. "Worried?"

"Should I be?" he asked and held my gaze in return. "I really like her, Sammy."

I tried not to feel each of his words like a blade slicing through my skin. I reminded myself that I was moving on, that it was only for the best that Max was finally finding someone to spend time with—and that Stephanie was a great match for him.

"What do you think I'm telling her?" I asked quietly and lowered my eyes.

"Maybe about my—" He cleared his throat. "—history."

"About you flipping through women like the pages in a book?"

"That's not fair."

"She's my friend, Max," I said. "You can't expect me to stand by and watch her get hurt."

"How can you say that?" His voice was getting louder by the second.

I studied him intently. It wasn't often that Max was truly angry with me, but he seemed to be getting to that point.

"I'm not going to hurt her."

"So, then you're ready to commit to her?" I asked. "You're ready to plan another date before parting ways?"

Max rubbed his hands slowly along his knees and shook his head. "I'd like to be. I'm trying. Doesn't that count for anything?"

"Sure it does," I said and shifted the melting vegetables on my knees.

I looked at Max—his beautiful face—those bottomless hazel eyes—and I remembered something.

I might have been harboring a crush on this man for years, but that didn't change the fact that this was my best friend. He was confiding in me, and all I was thinking about was how soft and sensual his lips looked when he pouted.

The realization snapped me out of my state of self-pity. Max had a real chance to be with an amazing woman and I was doing my best to ignore it, instead of giving him good advice.

"Actually, Max, that's complete crap," I said as I sat back on the couch.

"Excuse me?" He looked over at me.

"It doesn't count at all," I said firmly. "If you really care about Stephanie, then trying doesn't count at all. You just have to do it. No more hesitating. No more finding flaws that don't exist. She's is an amazing and wonderful woman and she shouldn't be toyed with."

"Well, that's a little harsh," he muttered. "I wouldn't say that I'm toying with her."

"What do you call treating a woman so kindly and then ignoring her attempts to get closer to you? Because I call it a bait and switch," I said with more ice in my voice than I had intended.

Max stared at me, his lips slightly parted, his eyes darkened with hurt. The innocence was gone now. I realized that.

"We're not kids any more, Max," I reminded him. "Just because you have a fancy job and a fancy apartment, that doesn't make you all grown up. You're not grown up until you're willing to put yourself on the line for someone else."

"Listen to you—the expert," he said, sounding slightly bitter.

I held his gaze, not affected by the tone of his voice. "Yes, maybe I am the expert. I know a little bit about waiting for life to happen, instead of making life happen."

"More of that self-help guru BS," he mumbled.

"Believe what you want," I said with a shrug. "But don't come crying to me when Stephanie looks for a guy who has the backbone to tell her what he wants."

"Hey," he snapped. "I came over here for a little help, not to get torn apart."

He definitely looked angry now.

"But don't you see, Max?" I said as I patted the frozen vegetables on my knees. "Sometimes getting a little torn apart is exactly what you need."

"I guess we'll see about that," he muttered and wiped a hand across his face.

"Listen, I love our chats," I said with a groan. "But I'm pretty sure I'm not going to make it to the bed. I'd really like to just curl up on this sofa and pass out."

"It's okay," he said with a sigh. "I've got some thinking to do." He stared at me for a long moment before letting himself out of the apartment.

As I closed my eyes from exhaustion I was aware that I had just shoved Max right toward Stephanie, but surprisingly, I didn't regret it. Not in the moment, anyway.

EIGHT

By the third morning that I met with Stephanie, I was feeling much more on track. When we started off on our light jog, I didn't even get out of breath. I fell into pace with her without having to think about timing my strides.

We were halfway around the pond when she began to chat with me.

"I've been trying to figure something out."

"Oh?" I asked and focused on my breath.

"I know that you and Max are friends, so I don't want to cross a line," she said, talking effortlessly despite the fact that she was increasing her pace. "I have a really great time with him when we are together, and he seems to as well, but when it comes to planning the next date, he's always shrugging it off. Am I doing something wrong?"

I took a big breath. It knocked me off my rhythm and off my pace. Suddenly Stephanie was the same as me. Maybe not in her athletic prowess, but in her level of insecurity. She was as uncertain as I was, despite all that she seemed to have going for her.

"No." I finally exhaled and quickened my pace. "Max is difficult."

She fell silent as we both broke into a run.

I wasn't sure if she realized how fast we were going. I didn't try to slow her down.

I felt as if we were running from the same sensation—a feeling of not being good enough—and it was the same man who inspired it in both of us. I expected to be beside myself with jealousy, but instead I felt a certain sense of bonding and sympathy.

Max was an amazing man, until he wasn't, and when he wasn't, it was heartbreaking.

Finally, I had to slow down. I simply couldn't keep up.

I eased back into a mild jog.

It took Stephanie a moment to notice that I had fallen behind. Then she matched my pace.

"What do you mean by difficult?" she asked. "If I shouldn't be asking you about this, just tell me," she added quickly.

I felt a pang of guilt for my friendship with Max. I wanted to talk with Stephanie—to share all of Max's little quirks that made him hard to pin down—but I knew that my loyalty needed to remain with him.

"I just mean that he doesn't always make the best choices. I think he is a little afraid of certain things," I said as vaguely as I could.

"Like commitment?" Stephanie laughed and nodded. "That's pretty clear to me. I even told him the last time that we were together that the only real commitment I saw in his life was his friendship with you."

I smiled a little. I had never really thought about that as a commitment, but suddenly I realized that it was true.

"He just needs to meet the right person," I said quietly.

In the past, I would have added in my mind that the right person was me—that he just didn't know it yet—but I didn't feel the need to think that this time. I found myself hoping—just a little bit—that Stephanie might end up being that right person.

If it wasn't going to be me, at least I could like the person he was with, and Stephanie didn't seem to be the type to break his heart.

"I guess," Stephanie said with a frown.

I could tell that she was hoping I would spill a little more. I kept my mouth shut for the rest of our run.

As we completed our practice Stephanie reminded me about the marathon the next day.

"No flaking out," she warned me. "You've worked so hard, Samantha. You can do this. I know you can. It might seem scary, but everything does until you do it," she said and smiled.

I smiled at her and nodded. "Thanks. I'll be there."

I wasn't sure yet if I was lying or not. I wanted to be there; I just wasn't convinced that I would be brave enough.

Thankfully, I had the day off work, which would give me plenty of time to obsess about it.

I read back over my blog post when I got home. I read everything from my first entry to my most recent one.

I stared at the message from Blue. I was reminded that I

had to finish the marathon. I had to present that picture. I needed to prove to myself—and to the few people that read my blog—that I was going to do this. It wasn't just about some silly list for me. It was about how I was going to choose to live the rest of my life.

Single Wide Female—wide open to whatever the world had to offer. That meant showing up and doing my best, even if I did end up falling flat on my face.

NINE

The morning of the marathon, I wasn't exactly pumped.

I was terrified. I was certain that I would never be able to finish. I was going to embarrass myself.

To make matters worse, when Stephanie arrived, Max was with her.

"Are you ready, Sammy?" he asked with a proud smile.

"Sure." I nodded. "But you know it's my first marathon, so I'll just do what I can do," I said with a mild shrug.

"You'll do great," Stephanie insisted.

I bit back my criticism of her prediction skills.

"Let's line up," she said.

I followed her to the starting line.

There were well over one hundred people participating.

I was eager to get lost in the crowd. I glanced over the other runners, wondering if there might be anyone who would go as slow as me, or might not finish. I noticed with relief, that there was a woman who looked to be about in her eighties. Surely she would remain in the back with me. We could be dignified together.

When the race started, I began a quick jog.

Soon, many of the other runners were passing me by.

Stephanie disappeared almost immediately. I caught glimpses of her between shoulders and hips.

I glanced over at the old woman, who had fallen into pace with me. She gave me a smile and then broke into a sprint. She was soon at the front of the pack, and me—well, I was fairly certain that there was no one behind me, but I decided not to look.

About a half hour into the race, I was ready to collapse. I had no idea when it would be over, but I was sure it wouldn't be soon enough.

I no longer thought about the other runners. I didn't wonder where they were in the race or if there was anyone behind me. I didn't try to spot Stephanie in the crowd.

I only heard the sound of my own shoes striking the pavement beneath me. It sounded like my heartbeat and the throbbing of my muscles. It sounded like my passion being poured out of me.

I listened to that sound and let it carry me forward. Even as my legs screamed for rest, I listened to the sound.

I remembered what Blue had said in the comment left on my blog. Just make it to the finish line, snap a picture, and remember it forever.

At the time, I had been arrogant enough to think that was far too easy for me—that of course I would make it to the finish line. But as the sound of my footfalls filled my ears, I knew that if I didn't have that request drilling through my mind, I would have stopped long ago. I would have given in to my exhaustion.

Instead, a nameless, faceless, genderless Internet friend gave me the fuel to keep moving forward.

As I plowed on, I wondered how much longer I had to go. I didn't dare to look up. Instead, I focused on the value of every step I took, mostly walking with short jogs thrown in for good measure.

All of a sudden, I saw the finish line beneath my feet. I hadn't even looked up to see it. I'd had no idea that I was getting so close. Then there it was, beneath my feet as I crossed it. I heard the cheer of the crowd and looked up with a wide smile.

I saw Max with a camera in his hand. He snapped a picture of me and grinned.

"You did it, Sam," he said with pride in his voice.

I felt my heart swell. I was so happy that I was ready to throw caution to the wind and kiss him.

But before I could, Stephanie wrapped her arm around his waist and grinned at me.

"You did amazing, Samantha!" she said in such a nice tone that I couldn't be angry.

As I saw Max kiss her cheek and pull her close, I knew that I had to back away. I had to let what was blossoming between them come into full bloom. It made me feel sick to my stomach to think of him with her, but it was the reality I was faced with.

At least I had the picture. Proof. For Blue. For me.

Someone handed me a paper cup filled with water. I gulped it down. I felt my body ready to give out. I crushed the cup in my hand and tossed it in the nearest trash can.

"I'm going to lie down now," I announced before flopping down on the ground.

I could hear Max and Stephanie's laughter as I stared up at the bright blue sky above me. All that mattered was that I had made it to the finish line. All I could think of was how proud of me Blue would be. I didn't let myself worry about how crazy that sounded.

Max reached a hand out to me. "Get up, champ. It's not nap time yet," he said gruffly.

I took his hand and let him pull me up.

Stephanie was grinning from ear to ear. It touched me that she seemed so genuinely happy for me.

"We have to go out and celebrate," Stephanie said with excitement in her voice. "There's a nice place that a bunch of runners are going to meet up at. What do you say, Samantha?" she asked eagerly.

I stared at her for a long moment. I was waiting for one glimpse of what must be an alien behind her perky smile. In what world did someone run a marathon and then go out to celebrate? I was verging on the desire of never lifting my head from a pillow again, and she was ready to order drinks.

"I say, you and Max should go," I said and shook my head slowly.

"Don't be like that, Sam," Max pleaded. "You did such a great job. I want to buy you dinner."

"Rain check," I said and spun on my heel.

As I walked away from the pair, for the first time I felt relief that they had each other. I didn't have to worry about either of them pestering me to do anything that would keep me from collapsing into my bed.

TEN

As I made my way to my car, I wondered if I was going to be able to drive home. But I certainly wasn't walking. I settled into the driver's seat and slid the key into the ignition. I knew I needed to rest a little bit before driving, so I pulled out my cell phone.

It was still sinking in that I had actually accomplished what I had set out to do. As I flipped through recent texts, I received a new message from Max. It was the photograph of me crossing the finish line with his comment "Amazing!" sent right after it.

I stared at the photo. It wasn't a model moment, that was for sure. My head was down, my feet were dragging, my shirt was soaked through with sweat, but my shoulders were straight.

I was looking forward to getting home and putting it up on my blog to prove that I had indeed accomplished something I never thought I could.

As soon as I arrived at my apartment, I opened up my

computer. I had already e-mailed the picture from my cell phone so that I'd be able to access it.

I pulled up the blog and let my fingertips hover over the keyboard.

Until this point my blog had been completely anonymous. I was known only as Single Wide Female, or SWF. I hadn't included any of my personal information, as advised by my technical guru and neighbor, Kat.

But Blue had asked for a picture of me crossing the finish line, and I was so proud of my accomplishment, that I was willing to put it out there.

What did I have to lose? Who would recognize me when I only had a handful of followers and even fewer commenters?

I typed up my blog post, describing the blue of the sky and the sense of wonder that I had actually made it to the finish line. Then I felt a sensation of fear well up within me. This was the moment when I would shift my blog from anonymous to claiming my own words—words that I'd had no intention of claiming when I had first typed a post. I needed to feel as if the world was open to me—not just the world near me but the world as a global concept. To me, this was a step in that direction. I uploaded the picture with the caption "Just for you, Blue."

I smiled as I submitted the post. I was sure that Blue would see it.

Who was Blue? Was she a woman struggling with her weight and her life like me? Was she a young girl still trying to discover her place in the world? Or was it some tall, dark, handsome man, waiting to sweep me off my feet?

As a knee-jerk reaction, I edited the caption of the picture to include:

Now it's your turn... What finish line have you crossed lately?

Leaving the personalized note left me a little nervous.

Would I scare a loyal reader off by being too direct? Would the challenge be answered with a picture or a comment—or worse, would Blue just not write anything at all?

I wasn't sure what to expect, but I was hoping to have some kind of response soon.

I left my computer on as I went into the kitchen to make myself some tea. I wanted to savor my victory.

I did, but I kept checking my blog.

Finally, I decided to turn my computer off for the night. I was driving myself a little crazy with expecting a response from a total stranger.

I fell asleep still thinking about Blue.

When I woke up, I jumped out of bed—ignoring my sore legs—and instantly turned on my computer. I was hoping that Blue would have left a comment by now.

When I logged into the blog, I was happy to see the notification of a new comment. I clicked on it and found that Blue had indeed left a comment.

First of many finish lines you will cross, SWF, I'm sure.

Beneath the comment was a snapshot of one bright blue eye framed by thick dark lashes.

Something about the eye itself made my heart skip a beat. I could see so much in that one glimpse. But it wasn't enough. I wanted to see more. I was insatiably curious now.

I typed out a quick response.

After all that sweat and hard work, that's all I get?

I bit into my bottom lip as I awaited a response. I felt as if I was cyber-flirting.

Even though I didn't know if Blue was a male or a female, I pretty much didn't care. Blue had shown more interest in my feelings and my life than anyone I'd spent time with lately, so I was willing to embarrass myself a little bit.

Of course I didn't expect a response. But I was hoping for one.

While I was waiting for an answer, I walked over to the drawer in my bedside table. I pulled out a small box and took out the small folded-up piece of paper from inside it.

I carefully opened it up and smoothed it out.

I could now cross "Run a marathon" off my bucket list. I drew a pair of running shoes beside the item.

Next up was one that I didn't think I was brave enough to post about on my blog, and I certainly wouldn't be including a photograph as proof.

It would require significantly less clothing. And significantly more courage.

I smiled, despite my discomfort as I thought about it.

#6 GO SKINNY DIPPING

ONE

I watched the rain drip down the window, twisting and changing direction whenever it felt like it. I envied that. The ability to shift course without apologizing. That was the new me—or at least the version I was attempting to audition for.

I listened for the teapot to shriek from the kitchen. I had woken up to a rainy morning and a contemplative mood. Of course, the first thing on my mind was the list. I held it in my hand as if it was sacred. I had poured my heart and soul into it and was not about to let go of the progress I'd made.

So far, I had not regretted a single adventure, but this next item on my bucket list—it was challenging. Usually, the things on my list were things that were a little outside of my comfort zone, but not too terribly terrifying.

But this time, I was more than a little nervous.

I stared down at the list in my hand. I had never really thought that I would get this far, so to see that item glaring up at me was a little shocking. It was also a little invigorating. I wanted more than anything to do these things, and I felt a sense of pride for accomplishing what I'd done so far.

As I stood up to walk into the kitchen, I tucked the list into my pocket. I was still thinking about it when I took the teapot off the burner and set it aside. I switched off the stove and turned to grab a mug from a cabinet to put my tea in.

In the process of turning, I caught sight of something sliding underneath my front door. I raised an eyebrow at the piece of paper that glided across the tile floor of the entrance of my apartment.

It was intriguing, but it was also a little unsettling. It meant that someone had been standing outside waiting to push that paper under my door.

I walked over to it feeling cautious. I walked along the edge of the carpet, just in case someone was watching for my shadow on the other side of the door. It looked like a flier because of its bright orange color and its bold black text.

I waited another moment to see if anyone would knock. Sure, there were salesmen in the neighborhood. Sometimes they liked to attach advertisements to the door handle or knock repeatedly until someone answered, but nothing like this had ever happened before.

I reached down and picked up the flier. It was an advertisement for a meet-up group.

Bored? Looking for some fun? Look no further! We are a group of adults that enjoy exploring and adventure! Some of our activities include:

Parasailing

Bowling

Bird-watching

Extreme Biking

I raised an eyebrow at the last item on the list. I wasn't sure exactly what extreme biking was, but I didn't think I wanted to do it. The list continued on, and at the end it included an "etc."

I found it a little strange that the flier had been pushed under my door, but I figured that the advertisement was left at all of the apartments. Now that I had discovered what the flier was about, I felt a little silly for being so paranoid.

I carried it back into the kitchen with me.

I'd recently made a new friend—Stephanie. It was a little weird and awkward to make a friend as an adult. For some reason there was a barrier between adults that seemed to scream—"Nope, don't even go there." But Stephanie was turning out to be a great friend.

Unfortunately, she was also more than a little occupied with Max, my *best* friend—which left me essentially friend-less and working very hard to be happy for them.

Part of my journey was putting myself out there and meeting new people, so I decided I would check out the meeting. It couldn't do any harm.

But first, I needed to make a plan for the next item on my list.

I took my mug of tea over to the sofa and tried to picture myself skinny-dipping.

"It's a rite of passage," I muttered in an attempt to convince myself. "Almost everyone has done it at least once."

I cringed at the thought.

There've been times when I've been in the water and it had felt so amazing when the water washed across my skin that I wondered what it would be like to be completely nude. There had been times when I'd been in a bathtub and wished with all my heart that it was much larger. Pool, bathtub—there really wasn't much of a difference, right?

Knowing what was next on the list and *accomplishing* what was next on the list were two very different things. I was sure that I had to plan ahead for this one. I couldn't just show up at a public pool and dive in without anything on.

Well, I could—if "public indecency" was the bold twist my list needed.

TWO

As I sipped my tea, I thought about how I would pull this off.

There weren't any swimming holes nearby. It would take several hours for me to get anywhere near a lake that I would be willing to risk swimming in.

However, there were plenty of public pools, not to mention hundreds of pools in local hotels and motels. I could rent a room, then I could slip out in the middle of the night and go for a naked dip. I might still get arrested, but even if I did, I would at least have paid for a room. Maybe the arresting officer would admire my commitment to self-improvement.

I shook my head at the very thought of doing any of this. Maybe this was one item on my list that was far too big for me to manage. I didn't want to end up with a mug shot of myself as a result of trying to be more daring.

I knew I was obsessing. I could go back and forth for hours without making an actual decision.

Luckily, I was headed into work in a few minutes, so I

could get my mind off it. I had a feeling I was going to procrastinate about this for quite some time. I wanted to be the type of person that could just jump into things without an issue, but that was not exactly me.

As I headed out the door, I heard the sound of it clicking shut behind me. I felt a sense of security when I heard that click.

Lately, I had become much more aware of living alone. Maybe it was because I didn't have Max running in and out of my apartment whenever he liked it. Maybe it was because I had come to terms with him not being a romantic option for me. Either way, it had crossed my mind that I was spending quite a bit of time alone. So the group would be a good thing to get into.

As I walked the few blocks to Fluff and Stuff, I shivered at the lingering chill in the air. The rain had cooled off the day considerably. This made me even less interested in jumping into a body of water without a stitch of clothing on.

"Excuses," I told myself. Apparently I was fluent in them.

As I continued down the sidewalk I heard the sound of laughter from across the street. It was coming from the outside seating area of a small cafe where Max and I often spent lazy afternoons.

It was Max's laugh, but it was Stephanie sitting across from him. I knew that if they spotted me they would be friendly—maybe even invite me to join.

But seeing them together in that intimate relaxed moment hurt.

I hurried the rest of the way to the laundromat hoping that they wouldn't notice me.

When I reached the shop, the employee working the morning shift was eager to leave. I barely nodded to her as she hurried out the door.

I felt a familiar sinking sensation. I experienced it every time I realized that my best friend Max was never going to be my boyfriend Max. So many years had gone by with my barely even considering other men.

It's over now. I reminded myself sternly. *There is more to life than pining away for someone who is never going to notice me in that way.*

I sighed as I checked on the machines to make sure they were running properly.

There was a young woman shifting her laundry from a washer to a dryer at one end of the laundromat. She had headphones on and didn't seem interested in striking up a conversation.

I sat down on one of the wooden benches that lined the wall and ran my hands slowly across my cheeks. I tried to focus my mind on anything except Max.

It wasn't long before I was thinking of Blue.

Blue, whom I'd never met, but who had so much influence on my life. I had a feeling from the posts that he was a male, but I still wasn't one hundred percent sure—and even that didn't mean much. He could have been sixteen or sixty-three—I wouldn't know. All I had seen was a photograph of what he claimed to be his deep blue eye—yes, only one of them.

"What is so interesting about that washing machine?" Max asked as he walked up to me.

I had been so engrossed in my thoughts that I hadn't even heard him walk in.

"Nothing," I muttered in return with a small laugh. "Just thinking about some things."

"Oh?" he asked and sidled up close to me. "What kind of things?"

"Life." I shrugged.

I wasn't about to confess that I was thinking of him, or skinny-dipping, or Blue. If he found out what I was up to, two things would happen. He would laugh at me and he would insist on joining me.

"How's Stephanie?" I asked, hoping to change the subject.

"She's good," he said. He was still watching me, as if he knew that I was not telling the whole truth. "She said she wants us all to go out some time, so let me know when you're free."

"Oh, sure, of course." I nodded.

I didn't think the idea of sharing dinner with the two would be such a great idea, considering that I might vomit if he tried to kiss her.

Okay, so I liked Stephanie, I adored Max, and they were a cute couple. That didn't mean that I had to eat while watching them make lovey-dovey faces across the table at each other.

"I saw you walk past the cafe," he finally said as he sat down beside me.

THREE

I felt the heat of a blush rising in my cheeks as Max waited for me to answer.

"Oh yes, I was running late." I shrugged.

"Right." He kicked his legs out in front of him and crossed his ankles. "As if the Fluff and Stuff can't spin without you."

I shot him a look. "You're always making fun of my job." I was already starting to feel annoyed with him. "It's just as important as yours."

"I know it is," he said. "But I also know that's not why you didn't stop and say hello. Are you really okay with Stephanie and me dating, Sammy?" he asked.

"Why wouldn't I be?"

"Well, she is your friend and I'm your—well, everything." He winked playfully at me.

My stomach did that irritating little hopeful flip it had not been invited to do.

"Arrogant, that's for sure." I shook my head. "I'm fine with it. I like Stephanie and she seems like she can handle you."

"I caught that." He shot a light-hearted glare in my direction. "Well, she is nice—but I don't know."

"Don't even start," I warned him. "She's perfect."

"Maybe." He sighed and stared at the same dryer I had been staring at. "Isn't it funny how life just gets ahead of you sometimes?"

"What do you mean?" I stood up and walked over to a dryer to pull the laundry out that was ready to be folded.

"I mean—" He stood up and followed me. "—I had settled into the idea of not really finding anyone I could settle down with, and then all of a sudden Stephanie showed up in my life."

"Ah, yes." I nodded. "She surprised you."

"She did." He nodded.

"At least it's a good surprise," I muttered. "You could wake up and realize that you're thirty-two with no potential mate in sight and a best friend who makes fun of your job."

"I'm not making fun of it," he said. "Besides, you make fun of mine all the time."

"There's a difference between not understanding your techno job and teasing." I began folding the clothes from the load.

"Alright." He sighed as if he surrendered. "But that's not the point. The point is that you're selling yourself short. You have so much to offer, but you hide yourself away."

"I do not," I shot back.

"You certainly hid when you saw Stephanie and me."

"Oh, you're being silly." I shook my head. "In fact, I am going to a meeting tonight with a new and very adventurous group of people. I'm looking forward to it. So how is that hiding myself away?"

"I guess it isn't," he said, sounding a bit shocked. "I think it's great, Sam."

"Glad you do," I said, my tone still short. "Contrary to popular belief, my world does not revolve around you."

"I know that," he said with a slight pout. "Just don't forget who held your hair back after that night on the island—"

"We agreed not to mention that." I glared at him.

"Okay." He smiled innocently. "I'm on my way out of your way, but call me if you get bored with your new friends and need some Max in your life."

"I'll be sure to do just that," I said with a slight laugh.

As Max left the laundromat, I felt a little more secure. I'd been so wrapped up in him for so many years, that it was actually nice to feel that unraveling.

Of course, now I had to go to the meet-up group.

When I walked into the recreation center, I immediately thought about turning around and walking out. I had gotten a little worried when I'd realized the location was the basement of an old church, but I was determined to still give it a shot. I hadn't expected old folding chairs and stale coffee, but that was exactly what I walked into.

There was a small group of people gathered around a card table littered with abandoned tiny paper cups.

I personally found tiny paper cups annoying. They weren't big enough to have a real drink, which meant you had to keep going back for more. Then they started to get weaker from the liquid seeping into the paper. Soon the cup was on the verge of collapsing, usually before I even had the chance to quench my thirst. It irritated me whenever I saw them.

I liked to imagine there was a factory worker somewhere questioning their life choices as they manufactured disappointment in cup form.

"Hello, welcome," a man said eagerly as he walked up to me.

He looked a few years older than me, but his clothing appeared about forty years older. He wore corduroys and a button-down checkered dress shirt. The combination made me want to take him shopping right that instant.

"Hello," I said with a small smile.

Now that I had been welcomed, it wasn't as if I could easily escape.

"We're so glad you're here." A woman with long brown hair smiled dreamily as she came over to stand next to me. Her voice was so calm and soothing that it verged on eerie.

"Okay," I replied nervously and adjusted the strap of my purse. "I think maybe I have the wrong place—" I began to say. I was forming an excuse in my mind to retreat.

"You're exactly where you're meant to be. I'm Lea," the woman said, extending her hand.

Her voice drifted over my senses like a cloud of cotton candy.

I couldn't explain why, but I smiled at her.

"Thank you," I said. "I'm Samantha."

I could have clobbered myself for using my real name. I was still trying to think of a way to get back out the door.

"She looks terrified," a sharp voice said from beyond the card table.

FOUR

I looked up to see a man who might have been in his sixties. His dark hair was slicked back, further accentuating his receding hairline. A bushy mustache covered most of his upper lip. It twitched when he looked at me.

"I'm Pedro."

"Pedro," I said with a warm smile. "It's nice to meet you. I'm not terrified—this just wasn't what I was expecting."

"That's what everyone says when they come here," the first man who'd said hello to me muttered. "Why does everyone say that?"

"Maybe because the flier doesn't say a group of misfits with nothing better to do than drink stale coffee?" Pedro suggested. "Really, Miles, you need to be a little more honest on the flier."

"I am honest," Miles insisted. "It says refreshments provided."

"I think he means more about the activities—uh, forgive me, but this doesn't seem like a very adventurous group," I said as gently as I could. "I'm really looking to liven things up in my life. I just don't think this basement is where that's going to happen," I added, hoping not to sound too harsh.

"Oh, you think you know us already?" Miles said defensively.

Although he seemed to be puffing out his chest, I could tell that his heart wasn't in it.

"I didn't mean it that way," I said calmly. "I just meant—I need action in my life, something to shake things up. I have no interest in slowing down."

"She's right," the soft-voiced woman said. "We want to do so much, but we usually just end up drinking old coffee and talking about what we should do."

"Well, you seem to have it all figured out," Miles pointed out. "What kinds of things are you looking to do?"

"I wrote a list," I explained. "Some fun things, some challenging things—all things I thought I would never do."

"Like what?" Pedro pressed with interest.

I hesitated. I didn't think I wanted to tell them about pole dancing, running a marathon, or posing nude.

"I don't know—just things," I said quietly.

"Oh yes, that sounds *very* lively," Pedro said with a snort. "I think you're in the same boat with us—no offense. None of us are here to be bored, but it's not so easy to suddenly become interesting, is it?"

"No, it's not," I agreed with a laugh. "I think the more I try, the more I lose sight of what I actually want to do."

"See, you fit in just fine," Lea said with a clap of her hands. "Okay, brainstorm! Idea!" she announced as if she was an alarm going off.

"Lea, please." Pedro shook his head.

"There's nothing wrong with being excited about a great idea," Lea shot back with a frown. "Listen, why don't we all follow her lead and write our own lists. We can all go home tonight, write them up, and we'll meet back here tomorrow. What do you think, Samantha?" she asked with a warm smile. "You can be our adventure guru."

I had barely mastered matching socks. Now I was a guru.

"Okay," I said slowly. I knew that Max was going to ask about my evening. I didn't want it to be a total bust. "Let's try that," I agreed.

That night, I sat at my computer and tapped out a lighthearted blog post about the group I had met and the ideas we were trying to generate for our next adventure. I indicated that we might just have our first adventure the next night.

I waited a few minutes to see if Blue would post. When he didn't, I sighed and closed the computer.

With its glow gone, I was alone in my apartment again, surrounded by shadows.

I started to feel sorry for myself, but I knew what road that would lead me down. I didn't want my life becoming a series of lonely nights. I sprawled out on my bed, closed my eyes, and imagined what it would be like to have someone to share my adventures with.

The next morning, I awoke and checked my blog.

I was pleased to find a comment from Blue.

I'm sure it will be fun if you are there. I hope you have a blast. Think of this poor guy missing out on your adventure!

I took a sharp breath as I realized what he had revealed. Now I knew for certain that Blue was a guy.

How interesting. But I didn't have much time to think about it. My doorbell was ringing, and I was still in my pajamas as I trudged to the door.

"Breakfast," Max said in a demanding voice when I opened the door.

"Huh?"

"Nope, none of that," he said firmly. "You are not getting out of it this time. Stephanie has a table waiting for us at the cafe, and I will wait for you while you get dressed. I know you're off today."

"Then you probably know that I want to crawl back into bed for a few more hours."

"Oh?" he said in a smug voice. "Here I thought you were all about adventure."

I stared at him for a moment, then slouched my shoulders. "Alright, fine," I said and trudged off to the bedroom.

Once I was dressed, I returned to Max, who was still waiting by the door.

FIVE

As Max and I began walking toward the cafe, he glanced over at me. "How did your meet-up go?"

"It was great," I said with maximum enthusiasm. "In fact, I'm getting together with them again tonight."

"Oh really?" He nodded. "Sounds like you must have had a good time."

"I did," I said with a smile. "I think that we're going to share a lot of adventures."

"Good." He held the door to the cafe open for me. "Just remember that being adventurous doesn't mean being dangerous."

"Thanks, Dad," I muttered.

He shot me a look, but was distracted by Stephanie waving us over to the table.

"Samantha! It's so good to see you." She gave me a quick hug.

"You too." I managed an awkward hug.

I sat down at the table.

Stephanie and Max leaned toward each other. Stephanie went in for a kiss on the lips, Max left a peck on her cheek.

I had to look away to keep from grinning. The two were obviously as uncomfortable as I was.

"Did you order yet?" Max asked.

"No, I figured we'd wait and see what Sammy wanted," Stephanie said.

Max and I both stared at her.

"What?" she asked nervously.

"You called her Sammy," Max said. "Only *I* call her Sammy."

"Oh," Stephanie said as she looked between us. "Sorry..." She frowned.

"You can call me Sammy if you want," I said laughing.

"Is that okay with you, Max?" Stephanie asked with a hint of suspicion in her voice.

Max grimaced, but nodded. "Sure, you know—it's just an old habit."

"What can I get for you?" the waitress asked when she walked over.

"I'll have a coffee black with a bagel—toasted, with cream cheese. She'll have a coffee—two creams, one sugar—and an apple fritter." He paused a moment and looked over at Stephanie. "What would you like, hon?"

Stephanie was gawking at him in disbelief.

I lowered my eyes. Breakfast had officially entered the danger zone.

"I'll have a coffee to go," Stephanie said with narrowed eyes.

"What?" Max asked.

"Why don't I just come back?" the waitress said, obviously sensing the weird dynamic.

"What's the problem?" Max asked Stephanie.

"Max, it's not really polite to order for me when Stephanie is here," I attempted to explain.

"Or that he seems to have a pet name for you and knows every detail of what you eat and drink," Stephanie added. She shook her head. "I knew this was too good to be true. If there was something between you, you should have told me before I got in the middle of it."

"Wait—you've got it all wrong. Max and I have been best friends for fourteen years—we've just become a big part of each other's lives."

"Or like an old married couple," Stephanie said and crossed her arms. "Look, Samantha, I love having you as a friend, but I don't want this to get messy."

"It won't," Max insisted. "You're taking all of this too seriously. Sammy is always going to be part of my life, and I didn't realize that I was offending you by ordering for her. It's just a habit."

"Okay, but all of these habits add up to something, don't you think?" she asked as she met Max's eyes. "Isn't there some part of you that thinks there might be a reason for all this intimacy?"

I held my breath as Stephanie and I both waited for Max to answer. I wasn't even sure what I wanted Max to say.

He looked over at me, almost as if he was waiting for me to speak. Once more I felt the glimmer of hope within me.

Was this it? Was I about to become the plot twist?

His lips began to part and suddenly I knew that I had to speak first.

"Don't be silly." I laughed. "Max is like a brother to me. I've smelled his dirty socks and seen his hideous music collection. Trust me, you have nothing to worry about." I smiled sweetly as I looked up at Max. "I think if in over ten years of being so important to each other we have never shown interest in crossing that line, that's proof enough that there is nothing more than friendship between us."

Max stared back at me, as if he might argue the point.

I wasn't sure if I wanted him to or not.

But he turned to look at Stephanie and applied his charming smile. "See? Nothing to be concerned about."

"I'm sorry. I guess I overreacted," Stephanie said as she stared down at the table.

"Don't be sorry, it's okay," I assured her.

I realized that I was telling the truth. It really was okay.

In that moment, when I thought Max was finally going to ask me for more than friendship, I understood that it was too late.

I was already on my new path. I was already allowing myself to blossom. Max was the old Samantha's way of hiding from real relationships. Now, it was time to truly let him go.

When the waitress returned, Stephanie placed her order.

I found myself relaxing as we shared breakfast and chatted. I noticed Max looking in my direction more than once, but I did not obsess over what it meant.

When it was time to settle up, Max pulled out his wallet.

"Let me get this," he said.

"Thanks," I smiled.

"That's what brothers are for, right?" he asked and locked eyes with me.

I could tell he wanted me to say something in particular, but I was not interested in saying anything more.

"Have a good day," I called out to both of them as I left the cafe.

"Enjoy your adventure," Max called back to me.

SIX

I actually couldn't wait to get to the meet-up group. I was excited to see what lists they had come up with. I felt like my presence there had inspired them to be a little more daring.

When I arrived at the meeting, I found my three new friends sitting aimlessly in their folding chairs.

"Hi, guys." I was still riding my high of being officially free of Max's hold over me.

"Hi," Miles said glumly.

"Good to see you." Lea sighed.

Pedro didn't even bother to look up from his coffee.

"What's wrong?" I asked, feeling slightly concerned.

"We didn't do so great on our lists," Pedro admitted.

"Nonsense, I'm sure you came up with something wonderful." I sat down in the circle with them. "Let's see the lists!"

"All I wrote down was mini-golf." Miles frowned. "Well actually, glow-in-the-dark mini-golf. With all those monsters and black lights—it's pretty unusual."

"For an eight-year-old," Pedro scoffed.

"Well, we can't exactly do yours," Miles shot back.

"I don't think mine are that bad," Pedro said. He handed me the list.

I opened it up and read off a few of the items.

"Steal a car." I smiled a little. "Well, that's bold. Let's see —rob a store. Huh?" I looked up at Pedro and raised an eyebrow. "I'm seeing a theme here."

Pedro shrugged innocently.

"It gets worse," Lea said with a sigh.

"How could it?" I asked and then read the next item on the list. "Steal a cop car." I laughed a little. "Okay, Pedro, you should just call this list How to Get Arrested or Shot."

"It would be an adventure, wouldn't it?" He grinned.

I shook my head and handed the paper back to him.

"Really, getting arrested only looks cool on reality shows and in action movies. In real life, you get strip searched and people watch you while you pee," said Pedro.

"Oh no, I can't perform with an audience." Lea shook her head quickly. "Once I was in this bathroom with about thirty other people and I couldn't go because everyone was talking—"

"Okay," I said quickly. "Well, good thing we're not doing anything on Pedro's list then." I laughed.

"But we have to do something," Miles said.

"Sure we do," I said. "But it should be something fun—maybe a little dangerous, but not something we're going to regret for the rest of our lives."

"What we need to do is something daring," Lea said as

she brushed back her hair. "We need to shake this group up a little bit."

"Maybe we should do what Samantha is planning to do," Pedro said as he looked over at me.

I stared back at him with shock. I hadn't told anyone what I had actually planned to do, but I had made such a big deal about it that of course they were going to be curious.

"Uh, no. I don't think that would be a good idea," I said quickly. "It's more of a private thing."

"What is it?" Lea pressed. "You have to share with us, Samantha—don't hold back."

"I don't know." I hesitated again and looked between them. "It's not something that I think you would be interested in."

"That's even better!" Lea insisted. "That's what we need —something to shake us up!"

"Just tell us what it is," Pedro said. "We'll figure out if we're up for it or not."

I frowned as I stared at all of their eager faces. I was certain that they wouldn't go for it, so what harm could there be in saying what it was?

"Alright." I sighed and took a slight step back from the group. "But it's really embarrassing."

"Just tell us." Pedro rolled his eyes impatiently.

"Okay, okay," I finally said. "I have a list of things that I want to do. I've done some of them. But the next thing on this list is skinny-dipping," I kept my eyes trained toward the floor, as I could feel my cheeks burning with embarrassment.

"Oh—uh—" Miles stammered.

"Alright!" Pedro offered a sly grin.

"That certainly is daring," Lea muttered. She looked a little puzzled. "So that's completely nude then?" she asked.

"Yes, Lea." Pedro wiggled his eyebrows. "In the buff!"

"See, I told you, it's not really your cup of tea. I mean, it isn't even my cup of tea. But it's on the list." I grimaced. "How do you guys feel about playing some pool?"

"I think it's perfect," Lea announced.

"I think it's worth a shot," Pedro said.

"We should do it tonight," Miles piped up.

"What?" I asked as I felt things snowballing out of my control. "It wasn't really meant to be a group activity. I was just going to jump in and jump out."

"But it's perfect!" Lea said with excitement. "It can symbolize a brand new start for our group. Just think about the kind of people we will attract if we can be this bold—this much fun!"

"I don't know that it will really be fun," I hesitated. "I mean, I don't even know where we could do it without getting caught. It is illegal, after all."

"We won't get caught," Pedro said with a wave of his hand. "Cops have more important things to do than catch a group of nobodies jumping into a pool."

"Hey, watch that negative talk, Pedro," Lea said sternly. "We're not nobodies. We are everybodies."

"If you say so." He shrugged. "The point is, the cops aren't going to care."

"Oh, and I know the perfect place!" Miles said with enthusiasm. "There's an old motel right behind my apartment complex. No one ever goes there. It would be perfect! We could swim all we want," he said with a laugh.

"Are you serious?" I asked, my anxiety growing. "I didn't mean that we should do this. I just—"

"Please, just relax," Pedro said in a soothing voice. "You're around friends here, Samantha. Why not take a leap into the unknown with a few decent people instead of alone?"

"How does she know that we're decent?" Lea said. "We have to honor Samantha's fear. She's only just met us."

SEVEN

Fear.

There was that word. That was the word that I was trying to eliminate from my life, not bow down to.

I wondered if I could really do this. Could I get naked in a pool with a bunch of near strangers? I took a long look at them. Yes, Pedro was older. I was fairly certain that Lea was on some type of drugs and Miles had a strange skin condition, but I realized I didn't care about any of that.

They were people—whole and perfect as they were—and I didn't have any problem with the idea of seeing them naked. However, I did have a little problem with the idea of anyone seeing me naked. It wouldn't just be a brief moment—it would be a full swim—with frolicking.

"I don't know." I hesitated and lowered my eyes.

"Samantha, we can do this with you, if you let us," Lea said. "We can all be brave together."

I stared at her for a moment. Other people might have found Lea's perpetual positivity a little off balance, but I understood where she was coming from. I had spent enough of my life trying to find a way to be happy, without ever realizing that all it took was for me to just let myself be happy.

"Okay," I finally nodded. "But no group hugs," I warned them, laughing.

"Of course not," Miles said with an offended grimace. "Just how kinky do you think we are, Samantha?" He shook his head.

Pedro winked at me.

I stared back at him with shock at first, but the truth was, he was rather handsome. I found myself smiling shyly in return.

"So it's a plan?" Lea said. "We can all meet at Miles' apartment. What time?"

"Tonight?" I asked, again hesitating.

"If we don't do it now, we might not ever do it," Miles pointed out.

"Yes, ripping the band-aid off and all." Pedro nodded. "I think it's a good idea."

"Okay, let's do it," I said with a shrug. I was still thinking that I could just not show up.

"Let me write down Miles' address for you," Lea said. She scribbled it on a piece of paper, then she handed it to me.

"Let's meet around six," Miles suggested. "It'll still be light enough to have fun, but late enough that the people around should be busy with their evening activities."

"Sounds good." I nodded and tucked the paper into my pocket.

"I'm so excited!" Lea said and clapped her hands. "And

the best part is, we don't have to worry about what to wear." She laughed out loud.

"Good point." I grinned. "I'll meet you guys there. I have some things to do first."

"No flaking out on us," Pedro warned gruffly. "You better show up."

I raised an eyebrow and wondered for a moment if he'd read my mind.

"I'll be there," I promised quietly before retreating from the room.

As I drove back to my apartment, I wondered if I would keep that promise. I wasn't so sure that I could. It was one thing to go skinny-dipping alone, but with company, I didn't think I could do it.

As I sat alone in my apartment, I tried to convince myself.

This wasn't just about skinny-dipping. It wasn't just about water. It was about shedding the version of myself that never felt good enough. I wanted to come up out of that pool a brand new person.

That might have been super high expectations, but that was what I was hoping for. I could hide away in my apartment and wait for life to become interesting, or I could take a risk and do my best to make it interesting.

I opened up my blog and read over my previous submissions. I could see how I was becoming bolder with each item I checked off the list. If I skipped this one, I knew that I would lose that momentum.

I was going to do it.

I got a little excited once I had actually made the decision.

I only wished that I had someone that I could share it with. I contemplated writing a revealing blog post about my intentions, but I thought that might be pushing things a little too far. Instead, I made a quick post about the adventure I was anticipating. I talked about how sometimes you had to take big risks to gain true freedom.

After I made the post, I noticed that there were a few more views on my blog as a whole. I smiled. It wasn't as if I was a famous writer, but it was still fun to think that someone was enjoying what I'd written.

I put away my computer and took a deep breath. It was time to head to Miles' apartment. I thought once more about simply not going. But I knew that wouldn't be fair to my new friends. They were counting on me to be their fearless leader.

"Some fearless leader," I muttered as my heart raced. I grabbed my purse and keys before I could change my mind.

I drove to the apartment complex and spotted the empty motel and pool beside it. It looked like someone had been keeping the pool clean and tidy. The day had warmed up quite a bit, and I was actually looking forward to getting in the water—until I remembered I would be getting in naked.

Then I thought about reversing out of the parking lot and making a run for it.

Unfortunately, Lea spotted my car and waved at me.

I cringed and parked. I climbed out of the car and walked toward them, each step making my heart pound faster.

"Join us," Pedro called out happily and waved to me.

The entire group turned to look at me. I realized that there were quite a few more people there than what I'd expected.

"Who are all these people?" I asked Lea in a whisper.

"Oh, they just recently joined the group," she explained with a giggle of excitement. "Isn't it wonderful?"

It wasn't wonderful. At all.

EIGHT

I felt excessively uneasy.

Forget about me getting naked. I couldn't deal with the fact that I was surrounded by a group of soon-to-be naked people.

I wouldn't know where to look, how to stand, or if I could refrain from giggling.

"I don't know if I can do this," I admitted quietly.

"Don't think about it too much," Lea said. "Come over here. Take a picture with us."

I sighed and walked over to the group. At least everyone still had their clothes on.

However, as soon as the photograph was snapped people began shedding clothes. Not surprisingly, Pedro was the first one nude, and he jumped with a huge splash into the water. Lea only had a loose sundress on with nothing underneath, so she was the next one to take the plunge. One by one, all of the members of the group jumped into the pool and began splashing and laughing.

I was the only one still standing there with my clothes on.

"Samantha!" Miles called out. "Hurry! Jump in!"

I shook my head slowly. I was frozen in fear. I couldn't even imagine all of these people seeing me naked, or me swimming in the water with all their naked bodies. I just had not evolved that far. I just could not bring myself to do it.

I began drafting my internal resignation letter as fearless leader.

"If she doesn't want to, she shouldn't have to," Lea said sternly. "It's okay, Samantha," she told me. "You'll know when the time is right. You can be our lookout for now. Give a shout if you hear anyone coming."

"Okay," I agreed quickly. I felt some relief that they weren't pressuring me to get in. But I also felt like a complete wuss. I was the only one who had chickened out.

"Don't worry about it, doll," Pedro said as he hung out near the edge of the pool. "One day you'll be old like me and you won't care who sees what," he said proudly.

I smiled at him as he swam away. I didn't see his body as old or anything but perfect. But I couldn't seem to show the same kindness to my own. After a few minutes people began climbing back out of the pool and putting their clothes back on. They weren't willing to risk getting caught.

Soon only Lea was doing backstrokes through the water.

"It's amazing, really, Samantha," she said.

"I'm sure it is." I looked away as she climbed out of the pool.

"Oh, Samantha, one day," she smiled and suddenly she was hugging me, dripping wet and naked.

"Lovely, okay—thank you, Lea," I said and gently tried to push her away, but my hands kept going to the wrong places.

"Are you going to come to Miles' place for snacks?" Lea asked.

"No," I shook my head. "I think I'm just going to stay here for a little while."

"Okay." She smiled and reached out like she might hug me again, but I crossed my arms.

"Have fun," I said.

As Lea pulled on her sundress and walked away, I wondered how much the failure of this night was going to set me back on my quest.

It was getting dark. It was surprisingly quiet around the motel pool. No one had called the police. No one had been hauled away naked in handcuffs.

I was beginning to feel very disappointed in myself. I knew that I should have been more daring.

Now that I was alone, the water looked very inviting.

The item on the list *was* skinny-dipping. I never wrote anything about its having to be with other people. If I just took a quick dip—in and out—I could check it off the list.

I didn't think about it for too long. I just stripped down. I tossed my clothes onto one of the lounge chairs and headed for the edge of the pool.

The water was not nearly as warm as I had hoped it would be. In fact, just putting a toe in left me shivering. But it was either stand on the side of the pool stark naked waiting for someone to notice me, or hop in the cool water and hide what I could of my nudity.

When I heard footsteps approaching, I knew that I had

no other choice. I jumped right into the water. It splashed up against my skin and took my breath away. I sank beneath the surface and stayed there, hoping that whomever I'd heard would continue walking by.

When my chest began burning, I was forced to pop up out of the water.

I glanced around to see if anyone was still around. I didn't see anyone. Maybe the footsteps had been in my head.

I began to relax in the water. It felt amazing as it surged across my skin. I felt as free as a dolphin gliding through the water. There was such a sensation of peace that I understood why some people preferred to swim without swimsuits.

I was just beginning to feel confident about my choice when I heard a jarring sound.

I heard laughter in the distance.

Somehow, I just knew that it was about me.

I heard the laughter getting closer and closer. There was more than one person laughing. It sounded like a group of people. All of a sudden I had a horrifying realization. The laughing people were heading straight for the pool. The pool that I was swimming around naked in or more accurately doing my best to hide in now.

My heart was racing. I didn't know what to do. If I climbed out of the pool they were sure to see me. If I stayed in the pool they were sure to see me. I was stuck, and I knew that there was no way I was going to get out of it. I had yet again placed myself in a position to be mortified in front of a group of people.

"Why do I keep doing this to myself?" I moaned out loud.

NINE

The laughter got louder. I knew they hadn't heard what I said, but I was fairly certain that they would be laughing at me soon enough. Even worse, what was I thinking?

I was naked in a public place in the dark! What if these people were dangerous? What if something terrible happened to me, all because I was being stubborn? This was it. I was officially going to lose my mind.

I started to pull myself out of the pool, thinking at least I would have the chance to run. I looked over my shoulder for the source of the voices only a few feet away.

"Would you like this?" a smooth voice with a hint of an accent asked.

I looked up slowly to find a man standing beside the pool, holding a towel. He had his eyes averted from me, as if he was being respectful of my nudity.

"Uh..." I stared up at him.

"It's okay," he said firmly. "I won't look. But they will."

He tilted his head toward the college boys that were preparing to enter the pool area.

I didn't have time to wonder who he was or why he was there. I didn't have time to worry about whether I could trust him. He had a towel. Which, at that moment, made him the closest thing to a guardian angel.

I climbed out of the pool just as the young men were surging into the area. I felt my heart skip a beat as I reached for the towel. As if he could see the terror in my eyes, he swept it around my naked, dripping body.

I was startled by the strange embrace and took a step back, clutching tightly to my towel.

"Thank you," I muttered as I hurried toward the pile of my clothing.

The boys were jumping into the pool and hollering. All they saw was a woman in a towel, no different than they'd likely seen at any other pool.

"I'm so embarrassed," I said. "I never do this," I added as I gathered my clothes.

He held the gate to the pool open for me.

"Nothing wrong with a little adventure in your life," he said warmly as I stepped past him.

He was still holding the gate when I stole a glance up at him. I stared into his deep blue eyes and for just a moment I wondered.

"Actually, I think it makes you quite brave," he murmured.

Maybe if I hadn't been naked, in a borrowed or perhaps stolen towel–maybe if I hadn't been terrified of the walk to the parking lot where I could discreetly pull on my clothes in my car—maybe I would have asked him for his name. Or for his telephone number. Or for the reason why my heart felt like it had crawled up into my throat permanently.

Instead, I scampered off to the parking lot without even considering that he might want his towel back.

Once I had wriggled into my clothing, I sat back in the driver's seat of my car and laughed. I laughed so loudly that I was sure someone would hear me.

It had been hard, it had been risky, but I had pulled off skinny-dipping. And I had to admit to myself, that I might even want to try it again someday—when I could be sure that there wasn't a group of college kids headed in my direction.

Even after I arrived at my apartment, had a shower, and was settled down in front of my computer, my mind was still on the man by the pool. It was dark and I had only glanced at him. I couldn't really remember what he looked like, aside from those deep blue eyes. I did, however, recall the sound of his voice. It was a memory I hoped I would hold on to.

It might have been a strange thing to do, but now I had an experience I never would have had if I *hadn't* done it. I felt brave, strong, and ready to conquer the world. These little steps were making a big difference in my confidence.

I logged on to my blog and was ready to make a new entry, when I noticed there was a new comment from Blue on my last post.

So what adventure did you go on tonight?

I stared at the question for a long time. I recalled the way the man at the pool had spoken to me. I knew it couldn't be possible—it simply couldn't be. Yet, it made me dizzy with excitement to think that it just might be. In fact, I began smiling from ear to ear as I typed back to him.

Wouldn't you like to know?

I added a winking emoticon. I wondered if that was getting a little too flirty and then laughed at myself for worrying about it.

I began typing out my experience of the evening, though I left out the part about the college kids and the mysterious man with the towel. The towel that was now a souvenir of my great adventure.

I detailed what it felt like to be truly free in the pool, and how I had almost chickened out, but was so glad that I hadn't. I mentioned having a magical experience that I would treasure for a long time to come. I didn't go into more detail than that. I was trying to be careful about disguising my identity.

As I was about to close down my computer I noticed I had a few e-mails. I checked them to find that somehow my new group of friends had discovered that I was SWF.

I hope you don't mind that we advertised that you're part of our group on our website, and we added pictures of our adventures from tonight! We're hoping to generate more interest—thanks to your blog!

I stared with disbelief at the e-mail from Lea and then brought up the website that she was referring to.

TEN

On the website, they'd posted pictures of all of us standing beside the pool—fully clothed—thank God!

I shot back an e-mail to Lea explaining that I wanted my blog to be anonymous and that I'd appreciate it if they didn't mention it on their website.

I knew it was too late. I knew that all of that information was now flooding cyberspace.

I sighed and closed my computer. I had a feeling that technology was going to get me into trouble; it sure seemed as if it had.

I decided to pay Kat a visit and see if she could do anything to help.

When I knocked on her door, I heard loud music blaring inside. I knocked louder. The music shut off suddenly and Kat opened the door. She was breathless and looked stressed.

"What?" she demanded.

"I'm sorry," the words tumbled out. "Did I interrupt something?"

"Yes—obviously," Kat said with some annoyance. "I was right in the middle of attacking an invader and now I'm going to have to start all over again."

"An invader?" I asked with surprise. "Is he still in there? Do you want me to call the police?"

"No, don't do that," Kat said quickly. She grabbed me by the hand and tugged me into the apartment. "It's a game," she explained as she pointed to her large flat-screen television, which seemed to be depicting the interior of a real house.

"Kat? Kat, are you coming back to the game?" a voice called out.

I took a slight step back. "Someone else is here?" I asked.

"No." She laughed. "Well, not really," she corrected herself. She picked up a headset with a microphone attached. "Sorry, Boss, I have company," she said before turning the microphone off.

"Oh, playing with friends?" I asked. Somehow I had missed the entire video-game trend.

"He's not really a friend," Kat said with a smug smile. "We're pretty much in love."

"That's wonderful." I smiled. "Is he local or—"

"We've never actually met," Kat explained and then held up a finger. "Don't you dare judge me, Samantha. There's nothing wrong with long-distance relationships."

"Oh, I wasn't judging," I said quickly.

I absolutely was. A relationship with someone you'd never met sounded like a beautifully packaged disaster.

"Listen, it's much more common than you think," she explained. "Haven't you ever noticed how much easier it is to express yourself through e-mail? Or how about that guy I've seen chatting you up on your blog?"

"Chatting me up?" I asked. "What?"

"Blue." Kat smiled. "Don't act like you don't know exactly who he is. I can see how fast you reply to his comments."

"Okay, he seems interesting," I admitted. "But I doubt he's chatting me up."

"You're wrong," she said with a shrug. "But the point is, you can be more open, really get to know a person without judging them first. Isn't that what your blog is kind of all about?" she asked.

"You've read my blog?"

"That's not the point, Samantha—focus." Kat laughed. "Don't knock it until you try it. You can really meet someone amazing through online dating or gaming like I have."

"Okay." I nodded a little.

I had to admit she was right. I had opened up far more on my blog than I ever had to any boyfriend. I had been buzzing with excitement at the thought of the mystery man at the pool being Blue. Of course that was just a fantasy, but maybe it didn't have to be.

I had plenty of time, what with Stephanie and Max being occupied. Maybe it was time to try out dating again. What better way than to have the chance to get to know a man and have him get to know me, before we ever met?

"I think you're on to something, Kat," I said with a smile. "Maybe it's time to add that to my list."

"I think it should be," Kat said. "Then maybe you won't interrupt my date nights."

"Sorry." I cringed.

"It's okay." Kat shrugged. "But why did you interrupt it?"

"Actually, I joined this group and they took a picture and put it on their website and then linked it to my blog and now I feel like I'm tangled up in the World_Wide_Web and—"

"Oh boy." Kat frowned. "That *is* a problem. I can take the picture down and clean this up, but if any of your readers on the blog happened upon the link to the group's website, you should know that they're going to have a good idea of where you live and what you were up to."

"That's alright." I shrugged. "I only have like five readers."

"Oh wow, did I not explain that to you?" Kat asked.

"What?" I narrowed my eyes.

"Just because only five people are following you, that doesn't mean that only those five people have been reading your blog. Anyone can read it," she explained.

"Ugh, maybe I should take it down," I muttered.

"Don't you dare," Kat warned. "I can't wait to see what happens next. I'll just have to help you keep it a little more secure. But first, let's get you set up with a dating site."

As I was pulled into Kat's world of technology again, I wondered if this would really be the way I would meet my Mr. Right.

At this point, I was officially done playing it safe.

Continue Sammy's journey...

Single Wide Female: The Bucket List
6 Book Bundle (Books 7-12)

#7 START ONLINE DATING — PREVIEW

Chapter 1

The wheels on my computer chair were making a quiet squeaking sound as I rocked from side to side. My neighbor Kat tapped away on the keyboard in front of her. Squeak, tap, squeak, tap.

"Samantha!" Kat said. She looked at me with annoyance, which was only made more dramatic by her heavy eye make-up.

"What?" I asked.

"I'm trying to work here," she said. "Do you want your profile completed or not?"

"I guess."

I had been avoiding completing my online dating profile for a long time, but now it was time to tick the item off of my bucket list. I wasn't going to meet the man of my dreams unless I started putting myself out there.

Stepping into the world of technology with my blog was a big change for me, but this was even worse. I was not only going to be exposed to anyone who had an account with the dating site, I was basically asking for attention.

"Do you want a date or not?" Kat asked. From the tension in her lips I could tell that she was getting annoyed.

"I do, I just don't know if this is the right way to go about it. I mean, who are these men that will respond to me? Will I even get any responses?" I asked.

"Oh, you'll get responses," Kat said. "You just have to worry about whether you'll get any decent responses."

"What do you mean?" I asked. I leaned over her shoulder to look at the screen while she sorted through some of the profiles.

"Look at this guy. He looks good on the surface—clean-cut, cute enough," Kat said.

"He looks good to me."

"But when you read his profile, you have to read between the lines. He says he's close to his family—which means he probably lives with his mother. He wants someone he can have a spiritual connection with. That means he's into open relationships and wants to have a spiritual connection with as many women as possible," Kat said.

"That's not what it says at all. How do you know that's what it means?" I asked.

"Trust me, I know." Kat rolled her eyes and flipped through a few more profiles. "I've been through enough of the duds to know them within the first sentence of their profile."

"Who are the duds?" I asked.

"Guys who have a passion for art and literature are comic book addicts. Then there are the relationship junkies who have been married at least three times in the last ten years. Some list their pets as kids," Kat said.

"I think that's sweet. Nothing wrong with loving your pet like it's part of your family," I said.

"There is something wrong with having to take Fido everywhere you go, along with his little baggie of poop," Kat said. She scrunched up her nose at the idea. "I dated this one guy who would inspect it before he bagged it. He said it was to make sure that the dog was healthy. Seriously, he would dissect it with a stick."

"Ugh, now that's pretty bad." I was already squeamish about the dating profile, but Kat's description of the dog-poop-toting date was enough to make me feel even worse.

"That's why you have to be choosy about how you select," Kat said. "This isn't about being nice. You have to weed out the dangerous ones too."

"Dangerous ones?" I asked.

"Sure, there are just as many creeps out there as there are decent guys. That's why you have to be careful. Always arrange your date at a public place, and always make sure that you tell someone where you are going and who you are going with," Kat said.

"Wow, this is sounding more like espionage than dating," I said. I sat back in my chair and sighed. "Dating was so much easier when we were younger. Maybe you hooked up with someone in high school. Maybe your college roommate had a brother."

"Okay, it might have been easier, but you have to look at it this way. By setting up a profile online you're jumping into a dating pool. You're surrounded by men who actually want a girlfriend, who are the type that you want, and who you'd probably never meet on your own," she said.

"I guess you're right about that." I started rocking the chair back and forth again.

"So are you ready? Can I hit submit?" she asked. Her finger hovered over the enter key.

"Wait, wait," I said. "You don't think I sound too cheesy? Do you really think that's the best picture to use?"

"I don't think you sound cheesy at all, and that is the perfect picture to use. Let's just do it!" Without waiting for my approval she hit the enter key. "It's live now, baby!" Kat said. "No turning back!"

I stared at the screen as the web page loaded and revealed my picture as well as all of the important details that had to be included in the profile. I felt extremely anxious, as I knew that now anyone could browse it.

"You okay, Samantha?"

"I think so," I said. My voice was a little shaky.

"Good, because I need to get going," Kat said. "Spend some time checking out some of the profiles that are matched to yours. You can always send them a message first, you don't have to wait for them."

"Okay, I will."

Kat left the apartment, and I was still staring at the computer in front of me. I wasn't ready to even begin looking through the profiles. I was contemplating deleting my own.

I got caught up in the search for much longer than I expected.

Luckily I had something to distract myself. Max was coming over for movie night.

Continue Sammy's journey...
Single Wide Female: The Bucket List
6 Book Bundle (Books 7-12)

BEFORE THE LIST

It didn't begin with pole dancing.

It began with a rainy afternoon.

A stranger under an umbrella.

And the moment Sammy realized she had been waiting to live.

ABOUT THE AUTHOR

Lillianna Blake writes uplifting, feel-good fiction about confidence, courage, and learning to live boldly—at any size.

Best known for the *Single Wide Female* series, her stories follow women who refuse to wait for permission, perfection, or a smaller dress size before chasing what they want. With humor, heart, and plenty of glorious mishaps along the way, her heroines prove that life doesn't begin after you "fix" yourself — it begins the moment you decide to show up.

When she's not writing, Lillianna loves travel, strong coffee, and stories featuring women who dare greatly.

Love Sammy's journey?

Get a free exclusive prequel and join Lillianna's reader community at:

LilliannaBlake.com

ALSO BY LILLIANNA BLAKE

Love bold heroines and laugh-out-loud mishaps? Explore more stories in the Single Wide Female universe.

The Single Wide Female Universe

Single Wide Female: The Bucket List

Single Wide Female: Holiday Fun

Single Wide Female in Love

Single Wide Female Travels

Single Wide Female & Family

Single Wide Female: Happily Ever After

Companion & Connected Series

B.I.G. Girls Club

Alex in Onederland

The Bride Tribe

Explore all Lillianna Blake titles on Amazon.

www.ingramcontent.com/pod-product-compliance
Lightning Source LLC
LaVergne TN
LVHW020531100826
845148LV00010B/1411